DEATH AND WEDDING CAKE

SUGAR CREEK MYSTERY SERIES

BOOK ONE

NOVA WALSH

CHAPTER ONE

Y ou can take the girl out of Texas, but you can't take Texas out of the girl.

It was a phrase I'd heard often, growing up in the hill country of Texas, but one I hadn't understood until I'd left my home state two years before to attend culinary school in the bustle of Los Angeles. Now, as I turned off the highway toward my hometown of Sugar Creek, I gazed at longhorn cattle grazing on rolling hills of bluebonnets and I couldn't agree more.

I was home.

An old Patsy Cline tune came on the radio of my rental car as I made my way through downtown Sugar Creek. It was the perfect soundtrack for a homecoming and I was glad I was wearing my sunglasses to hide the tears that sprang up. Memories flooded as I passed the streets of my childhood.

More tears came, this time spilling down my cheeks, as I turned down the lane toward the farmhouse where my older brother and I had lived with my aunt Meg after my parents died in a car accident when I was eight. After a minute, a sign hanging from an open gate to the right announced that I'd arrived. "*Primrose House, established*

2010" was printed in gold script with a picture of a wildflower field carved into the background.

A long dirt road wound through the trees and then gave way a moment later to a gravel parking lot dotted with cars. I pulled into a spot and sat for a moment, enjoying the sight of the big blue two-story house sitting on a wide green St. Augustine lawn. Even in the late April heat, flowers bloomed in full color in beds along the sides of the house.

After a nostalgic moment, I got out of the car for a good long stretch. Sugar Creek wasn't too far from the Austin airport—at least not by Texas standards—but I'd been sitting on planes since dawn, and my body was cramped six ways to Sunday. The air was fresh but warm and as the spring wind blew over me, the front screen slammed and a great big whoop came from the direction of the house.

"Why Abilene Anne Hirsch! Look how skinny you are, girl! I thought you went to L.A. to learn how to cook, not to look like one of them Californians! Get your nothin' butt over here and give your aunt a kiss!"

I had to brace myself against the trunk of the sedan to keep my balance as my aunt wrapped her arms around me and squeezed tight. She was a good head shorter than me, but what she lacked in height, she made up for with a bubbly energy I could never match. It was great to have her arms around me again.

"I missed you so much! I can't believe I've been gone so long!"

"Same here, sweetie. I hope the drive wasn't too awful. Sorry I couldn't come to pick you up."

"Oh, shoo," I said as I struggled to pull my overstuffed suitcase out of the tiny trunk. Why are rental cars always so small? "It was an easy drive and I know you've got your hands full."

"That's no lie, baby girl! This wedding might just be the death of me. What on earth was I thinking, saying yes to hosting this thing?"

The wedding, which was the main reason I was back in Sugar Creek, was set for the coming Saturday afternoon, and it was already Monday. The B&B hadn't hosted any events in the past, but when one of the local girls begged Aunt Meg to let her have her wedding in the backyard of *Primrose House,* she'd relented. And then promptly called me to beg my help with catering.

Luckily, I'd just finished up my time at culinary school and had two free weeks in my schedule before I was due back in L.A. to start a job at a restaurant. I'd gladly agreed to help out and get some much needed R&R back in my hometown.

I'd done as much planning as I could via email with Marlene Lewis, the bride-to-be. And if the planning was any indication, this wedding was going to be a major challenge. I'd gone to school with Marlene, but I barely remembered her. She'd been a couple of years ahead of me, so our paths hadn't crossed much. Our communication so far had been a mixture of Texas cordial and Bridezilla stressful. Between Marlene's high demands and the challenges of working in a small town and a small kitchen, I had my work cut out for me. But after the hectic pace I'd kept in L.A., I felt ready for it.

"Come on, Aunt Meg. You know this is a great idea. Just imagine all the business you'll get once the B&B is a proper event space. The hill country is just getting bigger, and the rich and famous are all flocking here to see and be seen. It's only a matter of time before *Primrose House* is profiled in *Travel and Leisure.*"

Between the growing popularity of the area's vineyards, the proximity to the state capital of Austin, and a well-run marketing campaign, tourism in Sugar Creek was increasing by leaps and bounds. The uptick in tourism would be great for my aunt, who already had a reputation as an excellent host. If we pulled this wedding off, I could foresee the B&B growing to great heights.

"I know you're right, honey. The question is, do I want the extra work?" She grabbed my suitcase out of my hand before I could stop her and marched toward the house. "Truth is, I'm getting old. I don't know how much more work I can handle. This wedding is already running me ragged."

I laughed, watching her bound up the stairs with my luggage. "You don't look too old to me, Aunt Meg."

She set the case down and waited for me to catch up. "Whether I am or not, I sure am glad you're here to help me this weekend. Not only can I use all the help I can get, you and I both know I'm no chef. Catering a wedding is *way* outside my comfort zone."

I gave her a warm smile, squeezing her arm in reassurance. "Don't worry, Aunt Meg, we'll get through this together. And who knows? Maybe we'll even enjoy it." Her laughter floated in the air, and it warmed my heart.

"We better get you settled in," she said. "I hate to say it, baby girl, but we're so full with wedding guests that I'm going to have to have you stay in my room until the wedding shenanigans are over. I hope that's okay! I promise I won't snore, though." She cackled as she walked inside with my suitcase, leaving me standing on the veranda of a house that once felt like home, and now held the prospect of a new adventure. I smiled, more at peace than I'd been in two years. It was good to be home.

———

Later that afternoon, once I had settled into my old room, Aunt Meg and I ventured back downstairs. She led me towards what was once our living room and now acted as a combination guest check-in area, lobby, and reading room for the guests. The walls were a soft periwinkle blue and white and lime green loveseats and cozy reading chairs dotted the room. Several vases of wildflowers in a variety of colors sat on pale wood stands and coffee tables. A huge bouquet graced the pine mantelpiece over the fireplace.

"Wow, it looks great in here! I love the new decor!"

Aunt Meg beamed. "Isn't it gorgeous? I couldn't have done it without Maria's help. She has a great eye for design and color. Speaking of Maria," she said and motioned toward the woman standing behind the check-in counter, "Maria, this is my niece Abby. Abby, meet Maria, my new part-time helper!"

Maria stepped from behind the counter and gave me a big smile.

"Hello, it's so nice to meet you! Mrs. Hirsch has told me so much about you."

Maria was Hispanic and looked to be in her early thirties. She had beautiful, long, silky black hair, and a dimpled smile. "I'm so glad you've come. It will be good to have some help in the kitchen. I have some experience, but only a little. I am excited to learn from you. I've heard you are a very good chef."

I blushed and shot Aunt Meg an accusatory glance. "Really, I only just finished school. But I'm excited for this wedding! I haven't been able to run an entire event on my own yet. We'll learn together."

Maria smiled and nodded. "Your aunt showed me the menus you've prepared. It all looks delicious, and I'm sure the wedding will be wonderful." She turned to Aunt Meg. "I finished preparing the happy hour foods and placed it all in the refrigerator. Is there anything else you need before I go home for the night?"

"No, no. That's fantastic. Thank you so much. We'll see you tomorrow."

After Marie gathered her things, Meg pointed me down the hall toward the kitchen. "Now, let's go see what you've got to work with. I'm sure you'll want to get reacquainted with the pleasures of a 1950s kitchen." She cackled as she walked. "I haven't changed it a bit since you left, unfortunately. It's the one part of the house I haven't had the time or money to fix up. There's plenty of room, but the amenities are probably far off the mark of what you've gotten used to with all that high-falutin' cooking you've been up to in the big city. Hope you can make it work."

"It'll be fine, Aunt Meg. Really, you should see some of the places I've had to cook. You'd be surprised."

"Still, I wish we had a better setup. If this becomes a regular thing, I'm going to need to renovate." She blew out a breath. "The current kitchen is fine for making breakfast and tea, but not much more," she told me as we moved through the old house, floorboards squeaking with our progress.

As we pushed through the door to the kitchen, the first thing I noticed was raised voices nearby, as if someone was arguing right outside the window.

"What the blazes!" Aunt Meg cried as she headed for the door that led to the yard and bolted out before I could stop her.

"Aunt Meg, wait!"

I followed her out, nearly colliding with her where she'd stopped in front of the door. I grabbed her arm to steady us both as two women standing in the yard turned toward us with angry glares. They were vaguely familiar to me, but I couldn't place them. Several guests crowded the lawn, watching the women argue.

"Sorry to interrupt, but I heard a commotion..." Aunt Meg began.

The shorter of the two women rearranged her face into a winning smile and came toward us. She was manicured and name-branded from head to foot, oozing money and confidence that made me uncomfortable. "No, *I'm* sorry, Mrs. Hirsch. Trisha and I were just...discussing the details of our arrangement."

The other woman had frizzy brown curls and long limbs. She wore cutoff jean shorts, a white t-shirt, and cherry red converse sneakers. She continued to scowl at the other woman through the apology. "You mean you were telling me how to run my business? I won't have it, Marlene. I don't care how much money or sway you have in Sugar Creek. You aren't in charge of me, and your stupid threats to ruin my business won't work. I'll move to another town and start all over again before I let your skinny butt tell me what to do."

"Excuse me?" the other woman huffed, the fake smile she'd given Aunt Meg and I quickly disappearing. "You and I both know that you agreed—*in writing*—not to be present during any phase of this wedding. That includes the setup. It was hard enough for me to agree to work with you, even with that stipulation, given the *history*." The woman blew out a loud breath, disturbing the blonde bangs that hung in a thick carpet at her eyebrows. "I knew I should have hired a company out of Fredericksburg."

"Well, it's too late for that," Trisha replied, a smile now creeping onto her face. "Good luck getting someone to do tents and chairs for a wedding your size on such short notice. Ain't gonna happen, honey."

Marlene, who I now realized was the bride-to-be in the upcoming wedding, nearly lost control. She began to lunge. But before she got her hands around Trisha's throat, a large man holding a stack of poles stepped from beneath the shadow of the big live oak shading half the backyard.

"Come on, Trisha," he said as he handed the poles to a teenager standing next to him. He moved toward the women, his hands outstretched like he was approaching a pack of wild wolves. "You don't have to do this. Why don't you just take off? Kyle and I can handle the setup. It isn't worth losing the business."

Trisha scowled another minute before waving her hand at Marlene. "Fine. I don't like the company here, anyway."

She turned and moved quickly toward a blue truck in the parking lot. Marlene watched her go with a smug smile.

"Thank you, Greg," Marlene said to the man who had interrupted.

"No problem, ma'am," he replied before quickly turning back to his work. Marlene patted her hands together and wandered off toward the front of the house without a word to us.

Aunt Meg turned to me and shrugged. "Guess it goes without saying, but that prissy one is Marlene, the bride-to-be. I suppose we'll do introductions later. Come on, let's go get some tea."

She headed back toward the kitchen and I frowned, suddenly wary of what I'd gotten myself into. I hoped this wedding wasn't going to turn out to be a big, fat mistake.

CHAPTER TWO

Despite it being late April, the A/C was blessedly cool after standing in the afternoon heat. I made a mental note to order extra ice for the event. It would be a hot one.

"What was that all about?" I asked Aunt Meg as we came inside.

"Your guess is as good as mine," she replied. "Trisha McBride was the woman quarreling with Marlene. She owns Wildflower Rentals with Greg Anderson, the man who broke up that fight. Trisha went to school with Marlene, I believe. But that's about all I know."

Aunt Meg moved to the refrigerator and pulled out a jug of tea and set it on the sideboard, grabbing two glasses from the cupboard and pouring us each a full portion over ice. I took a drink and sighed. Just the way I liked it, ice cold and medium sweet. Now I really was home.

"Whatever they were fighting about, I hope it doesn't go any further," I told her as I polished off my tea and set it down. "From my communication with Marlene I have a feeling we'll already have plenty of drama on our hands without anything more."

"You and me both, honey." Aunt Meg turned back to the fridge and began pulling things out. She handed me a board layered with sliced meats, hunks of creamy and hard cheeses, and dried fruit.

Then she pulled out a bottle of white wine, pulled out the cork, and placed it in an ice bucket. She opened a bottle of red and picked them both up and motioned me to follow her to the front room.

"When did you start doing this?" I asked her as I followed her out of the kitchen.

"Happy hour, you mean?" she asked. "This was Maria's idea too. Isn't it great? The guests have really enjoyed it. We get compliments all the time and we've seen an uptick in good reviews online since we started."

We came into the front room and found a middle-aged woman in a sundress leaning over the desk where Aunt Meg kept a reservation book. The woman jumped as we entered and straightened, before smoothing her gray hair and giving us a smile.

"What're you doing there, Janine?" Aunt Meg asked the woman. She set down the wine on a sideboard near the fireplace where glasses, plates, napkins, and utensils already stood, and I followed with the hors d'oeuvres.

"Meg, honey. How are you today?" Her voice was syrupy, and she eyed the food we set out like a vulture.

Aunt Meg eyed her warily. "I'm fine, Janine. And yourself?"

"Oh, just peachy!" She gave me a big smile. "Who do we have here?"

"This is my niece, Abby. Abby, this is Janine Yardley. She lives down the road at the old Stapleton house with her husband Frank. They moved in about a year ago. She likes to walk over and keep us all informed from time to time."

"If I didn't know any better, I'd think you were accusing me of being a gossip." She trilled a high-pitched laugh and, with an impish smile on her face, made her way to the wine and poured herself a glass.

"If the shoe fits, Janine."

The woman laughed again and took a sip. "You know you love it, Meg. What would you do without my gossip? You'd probably die of boredom out here with only the foreigners to talk to."

Meg frowned and looked behind her, making sure none of the guests had wandered into the room. "You know I love my guests, Janine. That isn't something to joke about."

Janine just laughed and shrugged, bit into a hunk of cheese, completely unfazed by the sharp tone in Aunt Meg's voice.

"Did y'all catch that catfight in the backyard a few minutes ago? My goodness! Nothing like a little drama to get a wedding going!" She picked up a plate and picked through the cheeses with tongs.

"Seems to me like it resolved itself just fine," Meg said as she adjusted the plates.

"I wouldn't bet on it," Janine laughed. "Those two are a fiasco waiting to happen. Y'all know the story, I suppose," she said with a grin. Clearly, she was happy to inform us.

"Word around town is that Trisha blames Marlene for ruining her life. I think that's a little dramatic, but..." she shrugged a shoulder and drank some of her wine. "Something happened between them during junior year, I believe. It started with a boy, as it usually does. Trisha stole Marlene's man. From what I hear around town, it's her M.O." She let out another trill of laughter, but her eyes were sharp and serious. She took another sip before continuing.

"But things escalated. One of them spread nasty rumors, the other made accusations of bullying. Finally, they were both kicked off the drill team. What I hear is that Trisha lost a fancy scholarship because of it and got stuck in little old Sugar Creek, mad as a hornet. Still single, too, if you can believe it. Marlene left as soon as school was done, got herself a fancy college degree and a fancy beau. And now here we are. Havin' a weddin'!" She popped a cherry tomato into her mouth.

Aunt Meg and I raised our eyebrows at each other. This sounded like a whole lot of drama. Not at all good for a wedding.

"I thought Trisha was dating that Blackburn boy, the one over in Fredericksburg?"

Janine shook her head sadly. "Honey, that ended months ago."

"How do you know all this?" Aunt Meg asked her. For someone so new to town, she certainly seemed well informed.

"Oh, you know, I have my ways."

"And how on earth did Trisha end up with this gig?" I asked. Surely Marlene wouldn't have hired her high school nemesis for anything having to do with her wedding.

"Trisha's company is listed under her partner's name and Marlene didn't do her due diligence."

"That must have been what Marlene meant when she said Trisha had agreed not to be present. I wonder why she went against her word?" I asked as I leaned over to snag a cucumber slice from the tray on the counter. Watching Janine make her way through the snacks made my stomach rumble.

"My guess is, Trisha wanted to poke the bear. Get one last rise out of Marlene. And hitting her on her wedding day is quite a poke! Ha, ha! I only hope it doesn't backfire. Trisha could be in for more than she bargained for, from what I've heard about Marlene."

Aunt Meg tidied the room with a frown on her face as she listened to Janine. I imagined all this drama surrounding an event that she was already majorly stressed about was uncomfortable for her. The room plunged into quiet as Janine continued to snack and Aunt Meg and I processed her gossip.

"Sounds like quite a bit of intrigue," I finally offered, rubbing the back of my neck, trying to smooth out the tension knotting there. The drama was quickly threatening to become a dense fog around the wedding festivities.

"Aunt Meg, is Marlene staying here at the B&B? I would've thought she'd stay with her parents."

"She's here, along with half of her family and all of her bridesmaids. Her parents moved to Austin a few years back. I know her husband-to-be is from out of town, somewhere on the east coast, I believe? They all rented a house down closer to town, but Marlene and the others decided to stay here. Like I said, a completely full house this week! Not often we get that kind of business, especially so early in the year."

An elderly couple wandered in for happy hour and Aunt Meg's face brightened. "Come on in, help yourselves," she told them as she gestured to the snacks and grabbed Janine's arm, angling her toward the front door. "Come on, Janine. I wanted to show you something outside. Abby can stay here and help the guests out, can't you, hon?"

"No problem," I told her with a cheerful smile. "It was nice meeting you, Ms. Yardley."

"Oh, it's just Janine, honey. Nice to meet you too. Glad you've come to help out around here. Looks like y'all are gonna need as much help as you can get!"

Chapter Three

A couple of hours later, after we'd closed down the happy hour, helped several guests check in, and had a quick dinner, Aunt Meg and I were sitting on the wide front porch in matching rockers sharing a bottle of Wild Hare Pinot Grigio from our neighbors to the east of us, and enjoying the last rays of sun, when a dusty red pickup pulled into the drive.

I barely set my glass down before a bubbly blonde jumped out of the truck and bounded up the steps, letting out a whooping shriek that sounded like a pack of invading marauders. "Abby!!" she yelled. Luckily, I'd stood up by that time because she ran right into me, grabbed me around the waist and started bouncing up and down. The few boarders who occupied the porch with us shot us uneasy glances.

"You're home! My best friend is home! Yippee!!!"

I laughed and jumped along with her, giving way to my childhood self for a moment as I hugged my very best friend in the world, Cassie Divine. Aunt Meg laughed and clapped her hands. "I couldn't wait to tell her you were home, Abby! I called her as soon as you got here."

"I came over as soon as I could. And shame on you for not tellin' me you were coming!" She let go of my body but squeezed the life out of my hand.

Aunt Meg stood up. "I've got a few things to finish up inside. Cassie, sit down and stop frightening the guests, girl! You wanna glass of wine?"

"Yes, ma'am, thank you." Cassie sat in the chair next to mine but didn't let go of my hand. "I cannot believe you have been gone so long! Lady! Why didn't you ever visit?"

"L.A. was crazy, Cass. I barely had a chance to breathe, let alone come home. It was classes during the day, internships and jobs on either side. I shared an apartment with two other girls in the program and I barely even saw either of them in the two years I was out there. But I'm done now!"

"Does this mean you're moving back?" she nearly squealed. She sat in the rocker Aunt Meg had abandoned, her leg jiggling wildly. Cassie had always had more energy than a football team, and it looked like nothing had changed. Aunt Meg came out and handed her a glass, then headed back in with a beaming smile. It was hard to do anything other than smile when Cassie was present.

I shrugged, sipped my wine. "I don't know yet. There's a job waiting for me when I finish this wedding up, and I still have my apartment out there. But L.A. is no Texas."

"Ain't that the truth," Cassie nodded and sipped her wine. "When I heard you were coming back, I was so excited! Woo! I asked Aunt Meg if you needed any help with the wedding and she said you probably had it covered but that I should ask you."

"I think I'm good, but I'll let you know. Aunt Meg has a part-time employee now and I plan to have her help with the service. Maybe in the kitchen, too." I smiled at her, so happy to see my old friend. "What have you been up to, Cassie? It feels like it's been forever since we've talked. Sorry I've been so out of touch." I squeezed her hand, and she smiled at me.

She settled back in the chair and sighed, cradled her glass in both hands. "I've got my own little place downtown now. It's a combo antique shop and cozy home. The shop's in the front and I live in the back. It even has room for a little veggie garden out back."

"That's great! What about your parents? Are they still around?"

She nodded. "Still in the same house, even. Mom's as feisty as ever and Dad's taken up some sort of Civil War reenactment thing since he retired. It's trying for us women in the family, but at least it keeps him busy!" She gave a big laugh. "Ty likes to help him out with it too, so I guess it's a way for them to bond."

I raised my eyebrows. "Ty?"

Cassie blushed and took a drink of wine. "I've been seeing deputy Ty Clayburn for about a year now. He's fairly new to town, so you wouldn't know him. He moved here from Dallas a while back, after you'd already left town."

"Cassie, that's great!" I gave her hand a big squeeze and leaned in, lowering my voice. "Is it serious?"

She looked out over the darkening field. "I don't know yet. So far, it's a whole lot of fun. But what about you? Find any hot stars to date out in the big city?"

I blushed and waved her away. "I've been so busy with school and work, I've barely had time to eat and sleep. No, I haven't dated anyone since college in Austin."

"Alan, right?" There was laughter in her voice, and I blushed again. "Alan, the pianist with the tiny little…"

"Yep, it was Alan. Tiny little apartment," I finished for her, throwing a glance toward the guests. She laughed at me and I took a healthy sip of my wine. "Honestly, I'm happy I haven't had the distraction of a man. Life is complicated enough without having to deal with a relationship. I can't tell you how happy I am to get home, but also how happy I am to have an actual break." I turned back to Cassie. "Tell me more about Ty. Where'd you two meet?"

"We started seeing each other after he came into my shop for a gift for his mama. He asked for my help picking something and, well, one thing led to another." It was her turn to blush. "I can't wait for you to meet him! Speaking of which, though, I've got to get going pretty soon. He's coming over to my place tonight."

I was sad to see her go, but nearly dead on my feet after my long day of travel and catching up. I couldn't wait to crawl into bed.

"Alright, but you've gotta come back tomorrow! Keep me company in the kitchen while I prep for this wedding, and I promise to feed you."

"Will do! I've got the shop open ten to five but after I'm done I'll head on over." We stood up and hugged once more. It was so good to see my old friend again. "Thanks for the wine, Aunt Meg," Cassie called through the screen door. "I'll see y'all tomorrow!"

As I watched her head back to her truck, a sense of deep satisfaction settled over me. I had truly missed my home, and I felt it more with every minute that passed. Or maybe it was the wine kicking in.

A quiet settled with Cassie gone and as dusk descended over Primrose House, I thought about everything I'd need to do in the morning. I wanted to take stock of what all Aunt Meg had as far as platters, cutlery, linens, and dishes and get whatever was missing rented or bought right away. Sitting down with Marlene to talk through the plan one last time was on my agenda too. I also needed to walk through the property and get a good feel for how the tents, tables, and chairs were set up so there wouldn't be any surprises when it was time for me to make my magic.

Just thinking about it all was enough to raise my blood pressure and I willed myself to save it for morning and relax while I could—a lesson I'd learned the hard way through one too many burnouts at prior events.

Aunt Meg popped her head out the front door, interrupting my thoughts. "I've got a few things to do before bed," she told me as she stepped out onto the porch, wiping her hands on a dish towel, "but help yourself to more wine or food if you're feeling up to it. Or hit the hay if you don't want to wait for me."

"Oh my gosh, I'm sorry! Here, let me help you!" I said and stood, feeling lazy and more than a little guilty.

"No, no. You enjoy the evening. It's been a long day, and you've got more than your share of work coming up soon enough." She bent and kissed my forehead before heading back inside.

That was no lie. Even though I'd prepared as much as possible for the wedding before I arrived in Sugar Creek, the real work was still ahead of me.

I pulled my legs up underneath me in the rocker and tilted my head back. It was good to be home, to see people I loved, to hear something other than traffic for a change. To just be still. It was a thing I'd ached for often without realizing it during my time in California. And it was easy for me to imagine how I might settle back here and make a comfortable life for myself. Life in L.A. was exciting, but empty. Nobody to share big plans or successes with, only the constant grind of trying to afford the life and stay ahead of the bills.

I hadn't made my mind up about where my future would be yet, but tonight my heart was beating firmly for Texas.

CHAPTER FOUR

The next morning I woke up before dawn, wanting to get a head start before the bustle of the morning began for the B&B. Normally Aunt Meg got up at 5:30 to start breakfast preparations for the guests, but I'd told her the night before that I would take care of it for her this morning.

I slipped into our shared bathroom and dressed in yoga pants and a tank top in the dark, careful not to disturb her, and then I headed through the house barefoot toward the kitchen, carrying my clogs in one hand, and my bag with my notes and chef's knives in the other.

There is nothing like having a kitchen to yourself in the early morning, before dishes pile up, before the work of the day begins. Aunt Meg's kitchen was clean and quiet as I turned on the lights, and I felt my mind wake a little more with anticipation of the day to come. Kitchen work could be exhausting, that much I had learned from culinary school, but even after the tough years I'd spent learning my craft, I still absolutely loved all that went into creating food for events. I loved the creativity of putting together a menu, the exacting planning to pull everything off, the crazy vibrancy of a kitchen in full swing, and watching the smiling faces once people tasted the food.

It was more than a career to me. It was a passion.

I got the coffeemaker going and then pulled my notebook from my bag and set it in front of a barstool at the counter. Then I placed my knife bag by the sink. The sun was just beginning to brighten the sky, and I stretched my arms above my head, coaxing more blood flow and alertness to come. The first thing I needed to do, I thought as I poured cream into a heavy purple mug, was to make a list. Lists were the only way I got through my catering duties. I depended on them for everything and I already had nearly a dozen for this job— what I would serve, timing and prep lists, shopping lists, lists of supplies—but what I needed now was a list of all that had to be done today. My lists would change and grow every day up to the event.

But before I started work on the wedding, I needed to get breakfast going for the B&B guests, which was always set out by 6AM. I shuffled around the kitchen, gathering everything I would need. The work was simple since Maria had made several trays before leaving the day before. She'd covered them in plastic wrap and left them in the fridge. I placed muffin and croissants along with fruit and yogurt out on the serving bar. Plates and cups were already in place and I set out two carafes—one of orange juice and one of sweet tea—beside the glasses and cups and whicker basket of herbal teas.

Once breakfast was out, I poured myself a cup of coffee and looked around the room, mentally working through the lists I'd made for the wedding so far. Oven space, or lack thereof, could definitely become a problem if I wasn't careful. I would need to do more precooking and then warming with chafing dishes than I'd originally planned. Other than tight oven space and a much smaller refrigerator than I was used to, I thought things would work out. I might need to rent a portable refrigeration unit, especially if the cake would need to be refrigerated. I said a silent prayer of thanks that at least I wouldn't have to *make* the cake. Pastry had never been my strong suit.

I sat at the bar in front of my notebook, pulled out a pen, and began to write.

1. *Pantry inventory and complete shopping list*
2. *Dish and cutlery inventory*
3. *Visit all local suppliers and secure ingredients*
4. *Meet with Maria and walk through her duties/skills*
5. *Finalized prep list*

I tapped the pen on the pad and looked out the kitchen window toward the lawn where the wedding chairs lay scattered about. Trisha's company, sans Trisha, I hoped, was supposed to show up by ten to finish putting up the tents and other rental supplies. I scanned the yard as I tried to think of anything else I needed to add to my list. As I did, my gaze fell onto a blue truck parked on the side of the yard in the grass. It looked like the same truck Trisha had sped off in the afternoon before. I hadn't noticed it when I looked out the kitchen window earlier, but at the angle from where I sat at the bar stool, I could see the side yard better. I frowned, not remembering the truck being there the night before. It made me angry that someone had carelessly parked where the grass might be ruined so close to an event. The last thing we needed was thick tire tread in the grass where people could fall and hurt themselves during the wedding.

Something was strange about it, though. I leaned forward and squinted to get a better look. The gate of the bed was down and a roll of light gray tent fabric jutted out the back. But there was something else that didn't seem right, something sticking out at an angle, not the same color at all.

My heart raced as I grabbed my clogs and headed out into the yard. I could swear that what I'd seen wrapped in the tent was a leg.

I stumbled as I hurried over the grass and got caught up in the rental chairs lying haphazardly about, the light of morning barely enough to see the yard and surroundings. I tried to make sense of what I'd spied out the window, but as I grew closer to the truck, I became more and more convinced that what I saw was indeed a human leg. One with a red sneaker attached. The ground was muddy, and I slid in my clogs. It must have rained in the night.

The truck was parked at an angle on a slope; the tent bunched to the left. And sure enough, a bare leg stuck out from the knee with a bright red converse on the foot. I yelped a cry for help as I grabbed at the fabric, frantically trying to pull the heavy rainproof canvas away from whoever was in the truck, wanting to free them from the confines of the tent.

It only hit me as I finally tugged the fabric of the tent free from the side of the truck that I had seen no movement from the leg. Because what I found as the fabric finally tugged free was the body of Trisha McBride, sheet white except for an ugly purple bruise around her neck. She wasn't breathing, and she still wore the clothes I'd seen her in the day before.

I cried for help again, this time at the top of my lungs.

CHAPTER FIVE

Aunt Meg had come running wildly out of the house at the sound of my screams, clutching a baseball bat, nightgown and hair flying. When she'd realized why I was screaming, she'd dropped the bat on the grass and run back inside for a cell phone and a bathrobe.

Now we stood in the yard and watched two police cruisers pull into the parking lot.

I shivered despite the quickly climbing temperature and glanced toward Trisha's dead body behind me. Guests had wandered out of the house, curious about all the commotion. It was only a matter of time before they made their way to us and spotted the body. I moved back to the truck to cover her with the tarp again to protect her from too many prying eyes, but as I did, I realized that something shimmered in the fabric next to her right hand. I leaned in closer and saw that it was a silver ring that looked like twisting branches, a dark blue oval stone set within the twists. Part of it was beneath Trisha's body and I couldn't see the whole thing, but I knew enough to not touch her now that I knew she was dead. Before I could look closer, I heard the officers behind me.

"Good morning, Ms. Hirsch," the tallest of the three officers said to Aunt Meg. The other two stood a little further back. "We got a call about someone finding a body?"

The officers wore brown uniforms and had very real guns on their hips. The one in charge wore a wide brim cowboy hat and boots. He was big and ruddy and handsome, with a long angular nose and brown hair that curled slightly at his ears. Stitched on his breast pocket was *Iverson*.

"That's right, Sheriff. My niece, Abby, found her." Aunt Meg touched the corner of her eyes, although her voice remained calm. It made me nearly tear up as well. I'd barely known the woman, but nobody deserved to die. Finding her all alone and just...dumped... the way she had been, it wasn't right.

"Hi," I said and reached out to shake his hand. The touch was electric, his big hand smooth and warm. I blushed as our eyes met and held. It took a fair bit of concentration for me to come back to the present, but I'm happy to say I could...after he dropped my hand.

"Sheriff Ryan Iverson," he said. "Pleasure to meet you, ma'am. Although, not under the circumstances." He gave me a friendly smile before turning a serious eye to the truck behind us. B&B guests were closing in now that the police had arrived. I saw Marlene in workout attire and full makeup near the edge of the crowd. It looked like she'd been up for hours already, although I had heard no one stirring when I'd been in the kitchen earlier. The house was large, but old, and sound traveled easily. Her room must have been far from the kitchen for me to not have heard her get up.

"Walk me through what happened, if you don't mind." Sheriff Iverson said as he ushered me toward the truck and motioned with his head for the other two officers to follow. I led them to the truck, but hung back as we approached. I'd already seen more than enough of Trisha's dead body, and I didn't want to get any closer than I had to. The sheriff stopped with me in the shade of the live oak, but nodded to his deputies and they started inspecting the truck.

"This morning when I got up, I saw this truck parked in the yard with what looked like a leg sticking out, so I came out to see what it was and sure enough, it was a leg! And I tried to get the tarp out of the way in case the person was stuck but when I got her free, I found her like this, all white as a sheet and not breathing, and..." I ran out of breath and he put a hand on my shoulder.

"It's okay, ma'am. Just take your time."

I nodded and watched as he pulled on gloves and walked to the bed of the truck. He reached for the tarp, revealing Trisha's still dead body. I closed my eyes a moment and took a deep breath before continuing.

"There was one other thing I noticed. I saw a piece of jewelry beneath her body, something silver with a dark blue stone. I don't know if it was hers or what." Stomach acid gurgled, and I willed myself to keep my coffee down. "That's about it, I guess. I didn't see anything else," I finished.

He reached to her neck and checked for a pulse, even though it was clear that she'd been dead a while, then scanned the bed and the tarp for anything obvious. After a minute, he motioned one of the officers. The man produced a camera and moved in to take pictures. I noticed he had *Clayburn* stitched on his pocket. Ah, Cassie's beau. I could see why she liked him. He was shorter and stocky but friendly, with a shock of red curls. I couldn't wait to meet him properly.

"And this is just how she was when you found her?"

"Yes, sir."

"And you didn't touch anything other than the tarp?"

"I mean, I probably touched her leg a little bit." I hadn't noticed at the time but the thought now made me woozy. I'd never even seen a dead body before, let alone touched one.

"And it was just you out here, when you found the deceased? You didn't see anyone else around?"

The guests, including Marlene, had moved in closer, and Sheriff Iverson eyed them warily. I thought back to the view from the kitchen, tried to remember if there was anything else I saw.

"No, it was just me. I was up early to do some prep work in the kitchen. I'm catering Marlene's wedding."

"That one was fighting with the dead girl yesterday! You could have heard them a mile away," an older gentleman with a balding head, obviously a guest, piped up and pointed at Marlene as the sheriff eyed the group. A couple of other guests nodded in agreement.

He glanced around toward Marlene. His eyebrows rose. "Is this true?"

Marlene looked around nervously and didn't meet his eye, as if he hadn't been talking to her.

"It's true," another guest replied. "I thought it would come to blows! They were mad as hornets, I tell ya!"

He frowned and then looked back at the truck. The deputy who wasn't Clayburn slipped on gloves and opened the passenger door. A few moments later, he came back around to us. "Registered to Trisha McBride."

Sheriff Iverson nodded. "Okay, do a thorough search in the cab. The truck must have gotten here somehow, and I bet you anything there's evidence in that cab if you look hard enough." The deputy nodded and returned to the truck. "So you found the body all by yourself," he said, turning back to me. "Did you notice anything you think is important?"

"Well, the, you know, the neck stuff." He moved to the body and examined the purple bruises on Trisha's neck. "Anything else besides that and the jewelry?" I shook my head, and he threw his gaze around the truck in a wider arc, looking at the ground where mud, my slipping clog marks, and tire tracks all disturbed the grass.

"Get plenty of pictures of the area around the truck," he told the officers. "I'll need measurements on any tracks you find. And call Dr. Lyman. Let him know we have a body for him."

He turned back toward the crowd. "I'm sorry for the inconvenience, but we'll need to speak with each of you briefly this morning. I would appreciate it if you'd all stay on the property until one of us has spoken with you. It shouldn't take long. And I think, if you're inclined, Ms. Marlene, that we will start with you."

"Oh, you can't possibly think I did this! Why on earth would I kill her and leave her here where it would ruin my wedding? That makes no sense!"

Sheriff Iverson's eyes narrowed. "You sure you want to do this here in front of everyone?" He gestured to the crowd, who seemed very interested in what Marlene had to say. "Or would you mind giving me a few minutes of your time somewhere more private? Maybe there's a room we can use inside?"

He looked at Aunt Meg, and she nodded. "Sure, you can use my office."

"I would be grateful. Thank you, ma'am."

"I didn't kill Trisha," Marlene whined. "This isn't fair."

"We are interviewing everyone present, ma'am. If you'd rather, you can wait until the end. But I think it would be in your best interest to cooperate, and quickly."

Marlene huffed and rolled her eyes. "Fine."

He motioned to the house. "After you."

After Sheriff Iverson and Marlene went back to the house, the crowd dispersed, guests shuffling back through the kitchen door in their bed clothes. I wondered how much mud we'd have to clean up. I put my hands on my hips and gazed around the yard.

What a mess. As if there wasn't already a heap of work to be done.

Aunt Meg gave me a gentle pat and told me she was going to get dressed and that I should take my time. I watched the officers for a few more minutes as they circled the truck, took pictures, and looked for clues. It was truly horrible, what had happened to Trisha. But I had faith in the officers. I was sure that they would figure it all out soon enough. I only hoped their investigation wouldn't put a damper on Saturday's wedding. Especially if Marlene had anything to do with it. If she really had killed Trisha, the wedding would be off.

It was enough to give me heartburn. The sun was already climbing high and sweat gathered at the base of my neck and on my upper lip. One thing I hadn't missed when I'd been in L.A. was the Texas heat. It would take me some time to re-acclimate. I wiped the sweat off my face with the corner of my shirt and then I silently wished the officers luck before heading inside to get back to work.

Chapter Six

When I finally came back to the kitchen, I found guests serving themselves breakfast and Aunt Meg pouring coffee. I assumed Marlene was still in the office with the sheriff because of the occasional outburst of Marlene's high-pitched whine coming from down the hall. Every time it happened, the guests in the kitchen would eye each other as if to say, *see, I knew it was her*. From the reaction to Marlene at the crime scene and the way the guests were acting now, it seemed like they had already solved the murder in their own minds.

I wasn't so sure. Marlene had a good point. Why would she kill someone and then leave the body in such an obvious location at the site of her wedding only days before the wedding would take place? Unless she really didn't want to get married and wanted to sabotage the affair, I doubted she would have done it.

Maria arrived a little after eight and Aunt Meg pulled her aside to let her know what had happened. She came back to the kitchen a few minutes later with red-rimmed eyes, shaking her head now and then and saying, "that poor woman." She refilled the orange juice and placed more muffins and croissants on the tray as I picked up my abandoned notebook and headed to the pantry to begin the inventory of dry goods.

I was happy to find a well-organized, if a little bare, collection of ingredients. Flour, several types of sugar, and other baking goods were present and labeled, but I noticed the spices were lacking, and probably old enough to need replacing. I put them on the list along with salt and pepper, which would disappear in a hurry when cooking for a crowd. The straightforward simplicity of the task kept my mind from my upsetting morning. It was nice to have something certain to do, something that I was in complete control of, unlike the situation in the backyard and what it meant for the B&B and the wedding that was supposed to happen on Saturday.

"How can I help you?" Maria asked as I came back out of the pantry with my notebook and a long list of necessary purchases. She was still downcast, although no longer teary, and I gave her a friendly smile.

"We need to count all the silverware to start. It isn't a fun job, but it's important."

She smiled and pulled out the silverware drawer. I removed the holder and placed it on the counter in front of her.

"Do you know if there's any more?" If what was in front of Maria was all we had, we were in trouble. It might do well for a dinner party, but we would blow through this amount of cutlery in minutes for a wedding.

"I think this is it, but I'll ask Mrs. Hirsch."

While she was gone, I turned to the dishes, counting dinner plates and salad bowls and tracking the numbers on a separate sheet in my notebook. It was a tedious task but a necessary one. The last thing I wanted was for my hard work in the kitchen to be derailed by something as minor as not enough salad bowls.

As I counted, my mind returned to the truck and Trisha's dead body. Someone had obviously killed her and left her at our B&B. But why? Had someone murdered her here at the house? Or was she killed somewhere else and brought here? And if someone had killed her here, why would they leave her in such an obvious place? It almost seemed like whoever had killed her had wanted her to be found quickly. I'd listened to my share of true crime podcasts, and normally when someone was killed, the murderer went to great effort to hide the body and cover up the crime. Why hadn't that been the case with Trisha?

Maria came back to the kitchen, interrupting my thoughts. "Have you been in Sugar Creek for long?" I asked her as she began counting knives. I rifled through the cabinets, pulling out every serving dish I could find.

"About a year," she replied. "I moved here with my daughter from Mexico."

"Do you like it?"

She smiled and nodded. "It is much better than where we came from. And my daughter is very happy at school. It took her some time, but now she has friends."

"How old is she?"

"Daniela is ten years. She is big for her age, and strong." She beamed with pride and it warmed me all over to know that mothers like her were in the world.

"It must have been hard moving here. Did you come with friends or family? Or all by yourself?"

"It was only Daniela and I. It was hard, but Mexico was harder." She placed the last spoon on top of the pile. "Forty eight spoons."

I blew out a breath. "Not enough. Not even close. Okay, thanks. I guess worst case, I can always go to Target and buy extra. But maybe there's a rental company. Actually, I wonder if Trisha's company rents kitchen equipment," I said, more to myself than to Maria. Although, I guess it wasn't Trisha's company any longer.

That thought led to a string of others. Was the rental company owned solely by Trisha? If so, what did that mean for the rest of our setup and event? Remembering the man that had stepped in to stop the argument the day before, I made a mental note to keep my eye out for him. I wanted to talk to him when he arrived and make sure we were still good for all the rental equipment for the wedding. And also ask him about what else might be available to rent.

A few minutes later there was a commotion as Marlene came flying down the hall, tears streaking her face, her hair wildly sticking out of her ponytail like she'd been gnawing on it. She ran upstairs to her room and there was a loud slam. The few guests who milled around quieted, waiting for what would come next.

Sheriff Iverson came down the hall and into the kitchen. He caught my eye for a moment and gave me a smile, making my cheeks flush. Goodness, he was an attractive man. I spun back to my notebook, but not before I noticed just how tall he was as he bent to speak to Aunt Meg. "I'm wondering if you have a guest list I might use, Mrs. Hirsch. It's going to get tricky trying to track everyone I've talked to, so if I could check it off to make sure I've gotten to everyone, that would be greatly appreciated."

"Of course. I'd be happy to get that for you."

She left the room and several guests rushed to him, hoping to be next in line so they could get on with their day.

"Do you know how much longer it will be?" a dark-haired woman asked him in deeply accented English. "I have a wine tasting appointment at noon and I really don't want to waste my vacation sitting around here. It would be fabulous if I could go next."

"Hey, I'm not here for this either! I should go next. I only get one vacation a year!" another guest chimed in. Grumbles began all around the room.

As the crowd grew restless, Sheriff Iverson held up his hands, placating the increasingly irritated guests. "I understand everyone's frustration, but please, bear with us. We want to move through this as quickly as possible too, but we absolutely must speak with every person who was present last night or this morning. A woman lost her life and we need all the information we can get. All I ask is a little patience and cooperation, if y'all would be so kind." His calm demeanor didn't waver, but I could see the strain around his eyes, the burden of responsibility weighing heavily on his shoulders. I did not envy the man.

The crowd quieted, and he motioned for the woman who'd first complained. "Come this way, ma'am. Let's get you taken care of. And as for the rest of you, why don't y'all make a list of people who have to be somewhere by a specific time and we'll try our best to get to you on time."

There was a bustle as he left the kitchen with the woman, and I turned to a clean page of my notebook and ripped it out. "Here, you can write your names and appointment times here," I told them, and stepped back as the crowd descended.

Just then, Janine Yardley came traipsing through the front door. "Goodness! Quite a commotion over here this morning! What in the world is going on? Why are the police here?"

"I'm surprised you don't already know, given your propensity for information," Aunt Meg said as she came back in the room with the guest book and a hefty bit of snark in her voice. It made me wonder if something more had happened between the two of them. It wasn't like Aunt Meg to be so snippy with anyone. I would have to ask her about it later.

Janine smiled. "As thrilled as I am that you think of me so highly, no, this time you have the drop on me, honey."

"Trisha McBride was murdered," I told her. "Someone left her body out back."

Janine's eyes grew wide, and she brought a hand to her mouth. "Oh, my goodness." She sat on a barstool, a look of shock on her face. "I thought those two cats just got into another fight. I had no idea Marlene was capable—"

Aunt Meg cut her off. "Nobody knows who killed her yet. The police are still gathering evidence," she said before heading out the door to give the sheriff the guest book and page of appointment times. I doubted half of them were real appointments, but I understood the urge to leave Primrose House. Truth to tell, I was feeling the urge to bolt at the moment too.

Janine shook her head. "Oh, this is so sad. Poor Trisha." She sank down into the stool like she was about to take up residence. "I bet y'all have had a terrible morning!"

I nodded but glanced around the kitchen, feeling mild panic at all I still had to do to get this wedding off the ground. Assuming there would even be a wedding. My manners told me I should stay and talk with Janine. But my duties won out.

"I'm sorry, Janine, but I really need to get back to work. I don't know much, other than that she died. Perhaps you can learn something from the guests?" Probably not the best idea to foist her off on our unsuspecting guests, but I really did need to get back to work. And the guests didn't seem to have much to do at present. Maybe it would keep them busy enough that they'd forget to complain about having to stick around.

Janine stood in a daze. "Of course you do, honey. Don't let me keep you. I just stopped by to see what was going on. No need for chitchat. I'll be on my way. You'll let me know if you hear anything else, won't you?"

She walked with me out of the kitchen and down the hall to the front, where she stood for a moment before turning back to me.

"Of course," I replied.

She beamed and gave me a little wave. "I'll do the same, honey."

I nodded again and watched her go out the front door. No doubt she would.

CHAPTER SEVEN

A few minutes later, Aunt Meg came back from talking with the sheriff. The guests, who were now spread around the front sitting room in various states of agitation, crowded around her and she waved for them to quiet down.

"Alright, I gave him our list, and he said he'll use it," she said and then paused, looking around the room at her dejected guests. "I'm sorry again for the inconvenience this is causing. I know y'all are here to enjoy yourselves, not to hang around this old house." There was polite laughter. "We'd like to make it up to you by extending happy hour tonight until 8PM. I'm sure my niece Abby, a fantastic classically trained chef who is gracing us with her presence, will throw in some fancy appetizers as well. Won't you, Abby? Something a little more special than the old cheese tray. As a token of appreciation for having to stay. A full bar tonight, too. Not just wine."

The room became perceptively more cordial.

My face flushed, but I nodded. I didn't love surprises, but her idea was a fantastic one. The last thing we needed was bad reviews because of this unfortunate turn of events. Anything to appease disgruntled guests and possibly turn the tide on the day was worth it.

My mind began working on what I might throw together. Mushrooms stuffed with local sausage and breadcrumbs came to mind. Perhaps puff pastry rounds with brie and jam or even my secret special artichoke dip I'd planned to serve at the wedding. Might as well test that out again on a crowd, see if it was still as good as I remembered it to be. Whatever I decided on would require a trip to the store, but I'd already planned to go downtown to visit the new gourmet food shop I'd seen when I'd driven through yesterday, so one more stop wouldn't be much bother.

Aunt Meg pulled me aside as the guests buzzed around. "Sorry to throw you into the fire, honey. But I really need your help."

"It's no problem at all. I can put something together."

"Thanks, love. You are truly a lifesaver."

She turned back to the guests and began answering questions. I headed to the bedroom to get my purse, but stopped as I saw Greg Anderson and a couple of his helpers pull into the parking lot. I hurried back to the kitchen, grabbed my notebook, and headed out the back door. Chances were high that if their company rented tents, they would have rentals for the other things I needed as well.

I wondered if anyone had told him about his partner being found dead in back this morning and hoped for his sake that he wouldn't stumble on her truck unawares. Surely he must know by now.

I slowed my step as I went down the path, and the sun hit my face. I must have worked in the kitchen longer than I realized because it was hot and humid, nearly midday already. It had been a rough morning, and I hadn't so much as sat down since I'd gotten out of bed. The stress of finding Trisha weighed heavy on me and I wished I had some time for a quick nap or even a snack.

As I squinted and scanned the yard looking for Greg, I saw that Trisha's truck and the police were still there. It must be hard on him to know his partner had died, possibly at this very house, and still come in and do his job.

After a minute, I spied Greg hunched over angrily near the trunk of a tree, his arms crossed at his chest as he talked to someone I couldn't see from where I was. But as I moved closer, I realized it was Janine Yardly, and that she glared at him with an anger to match. She leaned in and wagged a finger in his face, and he snarled back. But I was too far still to hear what they said to each other. As soon as they realized I was coming toward them, they stopped their conversation. Janine said one last thing that made Greg's face turn even more red before she hurried off in the opposite direction.

Hmm. I wasn't even aware that they knew each other, but I supposed a woman like Janine, being prime spoke on the gossip wheel, would likely know everyone in town. I wondered what they'd been talking about. Whatever it was, it wasn't a pleasant conversation. And not one they wanted to share. I hesitated as I approached, hoping to give him a moment to collect himself before I barged in on his thoughts. He turned toward me and I waved to him.

"Hi, Greg? We haven't formally met, but I'm Abby Hirsch. I'll be catering the wedding on Saturday."

The anger in his face smoothed over, and his shoulders relaxed. He was a big man, muscular but trim, maybe a little over six feet tall. I guessed he was in his late forties by the salt and pepper in his black hair and a hint of wrinkles around his face.

"Right, nice to meet you." He shook my hand and scanned the yard as if he wanted to get away.

Clearing my throat, I kicked at the root of the tree, unsure of how to say what I wanted to say. "I'm sure you heard about Trisha. I'm so sorry."

He nodded and the corners of his mouth turned down, but he gave no other sign of emotion.

I hesitated, not sure if I should say anything more. It didn't seem like a subject he was interested in talking about, so I moved on to the real reason I'd searched him out. "I wanted to talk to you about rentals, if you have a couple of minutes."

He brushed a large hand through his hair. "Yeah, sure."

"Does your company rent kitchen and service items too, or just tents and such?"

"We have some service items, but our stock is pretty limited. What are you looking for?"

"Mostly service pieces, chafing dishes, some silver, some bowls. I'll probably need a portable refrigeration unit. Cloth napkins probably too, but only in white or blue. I have a list if you want to look over it," I told him and handed him the notes I'd made that morning.

He scanned the list for a moment. "I can get most of this for you, but we don't have linens. There's a company in Fredericksburg that does that kind of thing, I think. I could get you the number if you need it."

"Oh, that's okay. I can find it myself. Well, that's a load off my mind. And you can get all this to me by Friday?"

He looked at the list again and nodded. "Should be able to." He fished a business card out of his wallet and handed it to me, along with my list. "This number is our business office. You can speak with our admin Stacy, who handles reservations and contracts. She'd have a better idea if we have everything you need and be able to make up a contract for you."

"Great! So you keep all your stock in Sugar Creek, or is it in Fredericksburg?" Mostly, it was curiosity to know how he ran his business. But also in the back of my mind, I saw Trisha's body wrapped up in the tent, and it made me wonder. Had that tent been here on the property the day before? Or had someone wrapped her in it before bringing her here? I wished I could remember the details of the yard from the day before, but I'd been so overwhelmed with my homecoming, I hadn't paid close enough attention.

"We keep all our stock in the warehouse over at my house."

"Everything? The tents and dishes and all of it?"

"Yep. I built the warehouse behind my house a few years back and it was the best business decision I ever made. Stopped paying rent, don't need to mess around with insurance for the stuff. And it cuts down on the time we spend going to and fro, since I'm already there. I can fill a rental request as soon as we get it."

"And you're certain you'll be able to deliver these things by Friday?"

He nodded. "It shouldn't be a problem. We'll be out to finish up the setup Friday morning, so I should be able to bring it by then. Or if that doesn't work, let Stacy know and we can tack on another delivery fee."

I nodded. "No, Friday morning is fine." My mind quickly turned to the problem of where we could store perishables until then, but I was sure I could make it work. Hopefully I could do enough rearranging. It would be worth it to skip a delivery charge, since we were already working on a very tight budget.

"Okay, thanks for your help. I'll give Stacy a call and set something up. And I'm sorry again about Trisha."

I gave him a smile that I hoped came across as sympathetic and he nodded, then turned back to his work. I headed back toward the kitchen to make a new list, this one for the evening's appetizers. Before I walked in, I glanced back. Greg was standing with his workers, poles scattered on the ground nearby. I couldn't help but wonder again, had the tent that wrapped Trisha's body been on our property? Or had it been at Greg's house? I made a note to talk to Sheriff Iverson about it the next time I saw him, or at least to Cassie, who could relay the message through her beau, Deputy Clayburn. Although surely the sheriff had thought of all these same questions. Still, it wouldn't hurt to ask.

CHAPTER EIGHT

My rental car was a hot steam sauna when I finally left Primrose House to run errands. I rolled the windows down and blasted the air conditioner for a few minutes before pulling out of the driveway and heading toward town. I'd been on my feet since dawn and it felt good to rest on the short ride downtown. After a quick scan of everything Aunt Meg had in her fridge, I'd put a menu together for the evening along with a brief sketch of what I would need to do and the timing, so I could get it all done by four. It would be tight, but I knew I could make it work as long as I found the ingredients I needed at the store.

Trisha's dead body flashed back into my mind, and my hands shook. I'd been so busy that I hadn't processed her death, and now that I finally had a few minutes to myself, grief settled in and the tears started. What a horrible thing, for someone's life to be taken in such an awful way. I didn't really know her, but I could imagine how terrified she must have been when it happened, how horrible to realize that death was upon you. I shuddered and reached for a tissue.

I assumed the bruise on her neck meant someone had strangled her. The muddy tire tracks hinted that the truck had arrived sometime after the rain had turned the yard into slush. I wondered what time it had rained and made a mental note to look it up when I had a few minutes. Not that I needed to know. It wasn't like I was working with the police. But something about being so close to it all, being the one who found her, made it feel important to me to figure out. I wanted to know what had happened and why so that I could have some closure. Not to mention that if Marlene really was a suspect, the entire wedding was in jeopardy. And what would it do for Aunt Meg's reputation to have her very first event cancelled? Even if it wasn't her fault, a botched wedding wasn't a good start to getting into the event industry.

Let alone a death on the property. But there was nothing to be done about that, now.

I wondered what possibilities there might be besides Marlene. Could Trisha have been involved in something dangerous? Janine had said she was single, but that didn't mean she didn't have a romantic life. I knew from experience those could be dicey. But I didn't know Trisha, and I didn't have a clue what those other possibilities might be.

I shifted focus back toward the tasks I needed to complete as I neared the small downtown. Sugar Creek was tiny compared to the bustling L.A. suburb I'd spent the last two years in, and the memories and sheer charm of the place brought a smile to my face and chased away sadness I'd felt for Trisha. There was a small collection of businesses on Main Street, a library and a grocery store near one end, a couple of antique shops—one of which was Cassie's—and diner style restaurants in the middle. Toward the far end of the strip, they had built several new buildings since I'd been in town last. A large national bank, offices, and new restaurants took up this space, and I noticed that two other buildings were going up at the far end. No doubt about it, Sugar Creek was bustling. It would certainly be good for Aunt Meg's business for the city to grow. I only hoped it would hold on to the small town character I loved so much.

I parallel-parked my car in front of one of the small shops and cut the engine, nearly giddy at how easy small town living could be.

L.A. had been a zoo, and it had regularly taken hours for even trivial errands to be done. This I could get used to.

My first stop was *Henderson's Fine Foods*. My plan for the wedding didn't require too many gourmet and hard to find ingredients, but I wanted to be sure I could get the freshest shrimp and a few hard to find cheeses for the passed appetizers. If I couldn't do that, I would need to make some adjustments to the menu.

The store was small but clean and well organized, one wall nearly full of assorted condiments, crackers, and other luxury pantry items. Refrigerators on the other side held a variety of fresh and frozen items. As I bent over a case of beautiful pies and cakes, a voice rang out from the back.

"Good morning," someone called from the back. "Be right with you!"

A few seconds later, my old high school friend Georgie Henderson came into the shop from the back. She was tall and blonde and seemed to have barely aged in the years I'd been gone. She carried a large box stamped "Refrigerated, Rush," but when she saw me she squealed and dropped the box on the counter, coming around to give me a big hug.

"Abby Hirsch! Wow, it's been a million years!" She laughed and squeezed me again. "You still in Austin? What are you doing in Sugar Creek?"

"Nope, not in Austin anymore. I went out to L.A. for culinary school. But I'm back this weekend to help Aunt Meg with a wedding at Primrose House."

"Marlene's wedding, yeah!" Her face turned dark, and she leaned against the counter, crossing her thin arms. "I heard somebody found Trisha's body out there this morning."

News sure had a way of traveling fast in a small town.

"I found her," I replied, feeling my hands shake again. I put them in my pockets.

"Oh, no! I'm so sorry, I had no idea!" Tears popped into her eyes and I felt bad for upsetting her.

"It's okay. It was a pretty big shock but I'm," I laughed a little, "I'm using work to distract me. Which is why I'm here. I wanted to see if I could get a few things for the wedding."

"Of course, I'd be happy to help." Her demeanor turned professional, and she moved around behind the counter and pushed the box out of the way, placing a pad and pen in its place. "Tell me what you're looking for."

"Crab legs would be fantastic. Snow crab if possible. And gulf shrimp. I have a list of cheeses I'd like too, or similar varieties, if these are too hard to find." I pulled a list of the cheeses out of my pocket and handed them to her and she looked it over. "Maybe some truffle oil as well."

"There is a delightful man from the gulf coast who brings me the freshest seafood by plane every Friday and he has fantastic shrimp. You're just in luck. I was about to put an order in to him, so I can tack yours on too. The cheeses shouldn't be a problem. As far as the crab, all I have at the moment is frozen."

"That's good enough for what I'm using it for, and I'm super excited about the shrimp! I'll probably need twenty-five pounds though, the bigger the better. Is that going to be too much?"

She waved my question away and wrote my order down. "No problem at all. I can get as much as you need."

I gave her a wide smile. "I wasn't sure what supplies I would find in town, but this is much more than I'd hoped. Sugar Creek sure has changed since we were kids."

"Things really *have* changed. With all the tourists coming in and wineries popping up every five minutes, it's barely even the town we grew up in. I'm happy about the changes, though. I definitely couldn't have opened this shop otherwise, but there are plenty of old timers who don't like it."

"That's the way it goes."

Georgie nodded. "And now I guess our town is big enough for murder. Who would've thought? I don't know if there's ever been a murder here before."

I shook my head. "I know, it's crazy."

"Do they know who did it?"

"Not that I know of, although they're looking into Marlene. She and Trisha were fighting yesterday, and people seem to think that's enough of a reason." I shrugged my shoulders. "Between you and me, I'm worried this wedding isn't going to happen."

Georgie frowned, and I noticed her glance down at all the expensive food I'd just ordered.

"Don't worry though, we'll take the food either way. Even if it doesn't work out, I'm sure there will still be guests to feed."

She nodded and put the pen down. "It sure is a shame that this happened now, right in time to ruin Marlene's wedding. She must be having a conniption."

"She wasn't very happy when the sheriff questioned her."

"I have a hard time imagining Marlene doing something as drastic as killing someone."

"I was thinking the same, but you never know," I replied.

"Trisha wasn't exactly popular in town. There must be some other suspects."

"I've heard why she and Marlene didn't like each other, but I wasn't aware that it was a popular feeling."

"She had a thing for other people's husbands, from what I hear. Lots of late night catfights at *Trevors*, that kind of thing."

It was the second time I'd heard this tidbit, and it made me wonder. "Do you know who's husbands, exactly?"

She frowned.

"For a while she was after Lyla Hornsby's man. But I think that was in the past, even further back than the man she was with in Fredericksburg. There must be someone new though, because I heard at church that someone saw her over in Blanco with a man from town. But no, I didn't hear which one."

Here was the aspect of small town living that I found distasteful, everyone in everyone else's business. It gave me pause, made me miss the way I could get lost in the big city a little. "But just because she's with a man doesn't mean she's with someone *else's* man."

Georgie laughed. "Why else would she be over in Blanco? That bird don't fly. Nobody goes to Blanco for drinks unless they don't want people knowing what they're up to."

It made me sad for Trisha, all the gossip flying around after her death. But I didn't really know her. Maybe she deserved the ill will.

She shrugged again and picked up the list I'd given her. "Doesn't matter much now, I suppose. But if I were Sheriff Iverson, I'd go looking for the person she was sleeping with. Isn't murder almost always a romance gone wrong?"

"Seems that way," I agreed, and then smiled. "It was so nice to see you again, Georgie. I better get a move on, lots to do today. But I am so excited that you can get the food for me! Let's catch up after all the wedding craziness has passed."

"Happy to do it! I'll give you a call when I've got the supplies ready, probably Friday morning. You want me to have it delivered?"

I thought about tacking on a delivery fee to the already massive food bill and shook my head. "I'll be by to pick it up. Thanks again and take care!"

"Same to you, honey! So happy to see you again! Hope you stick around a while!"

CHAPTER NINE

Cassie's antique shop was only a few shops down from Henderson's and after looking at my watch, I decided I had time to stop in for a quick visit before finishing my errands.

It was just as I expected when I walked in the front door, a pleasant chime ringing to let Cassie know of my presence. The floor was a light polished wood, and the walls were a buttery cream. Thoughtful arrangements of furniture pieces in all shapes and sizes filled the room, and shelves of smaller antiques—everything from silver spoons to vases and unique decanters—lined the walls. Where there was space, original artwork hung between the shelves and I leaned over to look at a particularly pretty oil of wildflowers while I waited.

"Abby! Hey, honey!" Cassie called as she came from around the counter where she'd been stretching beautiful red brocade fabric over a vintage chair that looked like a bear had mauled it. She set a staple gun down and gave me a big hug. "Tell me it isn't true," she said as she pulled me toward a pair of velvet wingback chairs near the front window and sat me down. "Tell me you didn't find Trisha dead this morning."

"It's true, unfortunately."

"Oh, honey," she cried and brought her hands to her mouth, shaking her head. "How terrible. For you *and* for her."

"It was horrible, Cass! Her body looked awful, there was a big bruise around her neck." I shook my head and closed my eyes, willing yet again for the image to disappear. "Somebody killed her."

Cassie's eyes began to tear up, and that got mine going too, which made me uncomfortable. I didn't want to go back in that direction, so I changed the subject. "But I did see Deputy Clayburn. We didn't talk, but he looks like a really nice guy." It was true, and it made me happy for Cassie. In my opinion, she'd never been treated as well as she deserved by men she'd dated. I hoped this one might be different, and I hoped he might help Cassie realize just how amazing she really was.

Cassie blushed and giggled as she wiped her tears away, falling back in her chair with her hand over her heart. "Doesn't he though? I'm lucky to have him."

"I'm sure he feels the same about you. I wish we could have met under better circumstances. He was there to do a job. It seems like they think Marlene might be involved. They questioned her quite a bit this morning."

Cassie's eyes shot up. "Right before her wedding? Why would she do it?"

I shrugged. "I don't know. It seems unlikely, right? What do you know about Trisha?"

Cassie sighed, leaning back in her chair. "Trisha and I didn't really run in the same circles. She was really into the dancing scene. You know I've always been a curl up with a good book kinda gal."

I gave her a big smile. It was something we'd always had in common, even as little girls.

She shook her head. "Trisha and I weren't close by any means. But from what I knew of her, she always seemed... I don't know, kind of sad? Like she was chasing something that would make her happy, but it was never enough."

"What else do you know about her? Did she have a house here in town? Is her family still here?"

"I think she lived in the apartments over on Ridgeway."

Not the best part of town.

"And I know her parents died a few years back. She has a brother, but he moved away."

Who would even arrange for her funeral? Would anyone attend? It seemed that Trisha was not well liked, and I felt a deep sadness for her welling up again.

Cassie glanced out the window, thinking. "I heard she was seeing some guy over in Fredericksburg for a while. But that didn't end well. Other than that, I have no idea about her personal life lately. We'd chat if we ran into each other around town, but that's it."

She looked back at me. "I wish I could tell you more. This is just terrible. Poor Trisha." Cassie squeezed my hand and looked at the hulking grandfather clock in the corner. "I should wrap up here soon. Want me to swing by the B&B after I close up?"

I nodded and stood. "That would be great. I need to get back and prep for this happy hour, anyway." I smiled and glanced around her cozy shop. Every inch had Cassie written all over it. "I love this space, Cassie. It's so you."

Cassie grinned proudly as she walked me to the door. "Aw, thanks girl! Hey, hang in there, okay? Don't let all this negativity distract you from what you need to do for the wedding. I have a feeling that it'll work out alright." She wrapped me in a big hug that I leaned into. Cassie Divine was one heck of a hugger, and it was exactly what I needed.

Chapter Ten

After I left Cassie's shop, I'd made a quick stop at the local grocery store, the ubiquitous Texas H.E.B., where I picked up supplies for the evening's cocktail hour. Best to focus on the work at hand. Cooking always took my mind off difficult things.

When I got back to the B&B, I headed straight to the kitchen. Laying all the ingredients out on the counter, I started mentally planning the cooking timeline. I'd start with the blonde brownies since those could bake while I prepped the other dishes.

I preheated the oven and grabbed a bowl and measuring cups. Sifting flour, baking powder and salt together, I mentally ran through the list of everything else that needed to be done in time for happy hour. I'd chosen appetizers that would feel upscale but not take a long time, but there were a lot of moving parts I needed to keep in mind.

Next, I whipped the butter and sugar together and then added eggs and vanilla before mixing the dry ingredients in. Just as I was pouring the batter into a sheet pan, Marlene and an older woman came into the kitchen in a huff. They were mid-argument and didn't notice me as they made their way to the coffeemaker Aunt Meg always had available for guests in the corner.

"Well, how on earth did your grandma's ring end up under a dead woman, Marlene?" her mother demanded. "I taught you to take better care of your things than that."

I busied myself tidying up, keeping my head down. They must be talking about the silver ring I'd seen beneath Trisha. Despite my best intentions, I craned my neck to listen in.

Marlene opened her mouth to reply, but then saw me. She pressed her lips together and grabbed two mugs, angrily filling them with coffee.

The older woman gave me an apologetic smile. "I'm sorry, hon. Didn't realize you were in here."

I nodded and smiled at them both, hoping to disarm the tension. It probably wasn't the best time, but I suddenly decided to be brave and introduce myself officially to Marlene. I needed to find a time to go over the menu with her, anyway. It's something I normally would have done before placing an order for food with Georgie, but there hadn't been time, what with all the morning's commotion. I figured there was still time to change my order, but only just barely. If I didn't make a move to talk to her now, there would be no chance to pivot.

I came around the counter and wiped my hands on my apron.

"Actually, I was hoping to talk with you for a few minutes, if you wouldn't mind. You're Marlene, right? I'm Abby. We spoke several times by email."

Marlene rearranged her face into something more hospitable and shot a quick glance at the older woman. "Of course, sorry we haven't talked yet. This is my mother, Beth. As you know, it's been a hectic day." Her lip trembled, and I worried I was about to lose her, so I pulled out a chair at the kitchen table.

"Here, why don't you have a seat. I'm sure you're exhausted. And I know now isn't the ideal time, but if you don't mind, I'd really love to go over the menu for the wedding and finalize everything so I can get the prep underway."

Marlene and the woman both smiled and sat. I'm sure they were happy for the distraction. "Of course. Let's go over the menu. I just hope there's still going to be a wedding for you to cook for at this point." Her lip trembled again.

I gave her a reassuring smile. "Try not to worry. Why don't we start with the passed appetizers and work our way through?"

I grabbed my notebook from the counter nearby and sat down at the table with them, flipping back a few pages to where I'd hashed out the wedding menu. I'd crossed off several lines over the last weeks as Marlene had changed her mind over and over. Yet another reason to double check with her before I went any further in my preparations.

"For the appetizers, we'd settled on crab cakes with mango sauce, a gourmet cheese spread, and my signature artichoke dip with crackers and vegetables. Does this still sound right?"

Marlene nodded. "That's right."

"And for the main course, filet mignon with red wine sauce, grilled shrimp, gruyere scalloped potatoes and honey butter carrots."

Marlene made a face, and my heart sank. *Here we go.* I knew it couldn't be so simple as to not have any changes in the last days before the wedding. It was never that easy, especially not with someone like Marlene.

"It sounds really heavy. I'm barely fitting into my dress as it is," she whined and glanced at her mother.

Quick thinking saved me. "We could do a pear and pecan spinach salad instead of the carrots. And baked potato rounds rather than the scalloped potatoes."

She beamed, and I sighed with relief. What I'd proposed would probably be even less work than I'd originally planned. And I wouldn't have to change anything I'd ordered from Georgie.

"That sounds perfect," Marlene said and stood up. Her mother did the same. "I just hope all this planning isn't for nothing."

I gave her a reassuring look. "Try not to worry. We'll take it one step at a time."

Marlene nodded. "Well, I appreciate you double checking. We'll let you get back to what you were doing."

After they left, I tucked my notebook away, relieved to have confirmed the menu. Though despite my reassurances, I couldn't shake Marlene's comments about the wedding not happening. What did she know about the investigation that I didn't?

It was all so strange. That the body had been left here. That the ring had been left with Trisha. It certainly looked like someone was trying to frame Marlene. I hoped for Marlene's sake, and for the sake of the wedding, that it was as simple as someone framing her. And that the police would find the actual killer quickly.

Relieved to have the kitchen to myself again, I quickly worked through the rest of the happy hour prep, sautéing sausage with garlic and herbs, then mixing in breadcrumbs and Parmesan cheese before stuffing the mushrooms, and then pulsing ingredients for gazpacho in the food processor with olive oil and a touch of vinegar until smooth. I exchanged the pan of brownies with the mushrooms in the oven and set the dessert on the counter to cool. They smelled heavenly, all caramelized sugar and gooey buttery sweetness.

After finding Trisha's body that morning, it felt good to lose myself in cooking for a while. Making delicious food always soothed my soul. Now it was time to see if the guests felt the same way.

CHAPTER ELEVEN

After a few minutes of setup, I was ready for the crowd. When I gave the word, the guests descended on my spread like a pack of wild dogs and began discussing their day in more and more jovial tones as the liquor loosened them up. Aunt Meg mingled with them, a big smile on her face, and I was happy my food had helped lighten the B&B mood some. Since she looked like she had it covered, I went back to the kitchen to clean up.

There was a sink full of dirty pots and pans that needed scrubbing, but thankfully Aunt Meg at least had an excellent new dishwasher. I loaded it up, wiped down the counters, and went back out to check on the guests and the food supply.

As I walked down the hall from the kitchen to the common area, I heard raised voices and picked up my pace. The mood in the room had changed considerably since I'd left. I looked around for Aunt Meg but didn't see her.

"It isn't fair," someone cried. "Marlene didn't do anything!" I entered the room and found a gaggle of bridesmaids guzzling wine and conversing loudly at one of the corner tables. Some of the other guests who were in the room eyed them warily. One foreign couple took a plate of food and silently slipped upstairs to the bedrooms.

The drama was no good. We'd wanted the happy hour to calm the guests, to erase the memories of the morning's inconvenience, not get them more riled up. And here was a group of women destroying all that. I looked around the room quickly and realized that it was up to me to run interference.

"Hi, ladies," I said with a calm smile as I approached the table. The maid-of-honor clutched her wineglass and tears streaked her face. "How is everything? Enjoying the food?" I noticed that only two of them had plates and that those plates only held a few pieces of broccoli and carrots. Not a dip or cheese or fattening morsel in sight. Ah, bridesmaids.

A couple of them nodded, but the maid-of-honor glared at me. "No, everything is not alright!"

"Patricia, please," another of them whispered to her. "It's not her fault!"

"Marlene's being investigated for murder! And the wedding is only days away. We should be thinking about hair and nails, not answering questions from the police. Nothing is alright!" Patricia wailed. I eyed an older man in the corner, the one who'd been the first to accuse Marlene of fighting with Trisha earlier. What was his deal? Rather than being put out at the noise, he seemed to be enjoying himself quite a bit. He had a dark beer in a glass and a plate piled high with food, a smirk plastered on his face as he watched the scene.

"I understand you're upset about what happened this morning," I told the group as calmly as I could. "But I'm sure the police are they're working hard—"

As if the gaggle of women making a ruckus wasn't enough, at just that moment Marlene breezed in, followed by a big blonde man who looked as much like a golden retriever as he did a human.

Marlene grabbed a glass of wine and flopped down on the sofa, the big man sitting on the arm beside her.

"Y'all will not believe what just happened to me." She gulped half her glass of wine and I bit my lip, wondering if I should go find

Aunt Meg, put a stop to the chaos, or just let it roll. Truth was, though, I wanted to know what had just happened to Marlene as bad as everyone else in the room. The shaggy dog of a man sitting next to her rubbed her shoulder.

Ah, this must be the groom. I'd wondered when he'd make an appearance.

"It's this whole mess with the murder. I went to get my hair done with Mama today, and Barbara Wexlar made some ugly comments about not wanting to be in the same place as a murderess loud enough for the whole salon to hear."

The man slid down onto the couch beside her and draped his arm over her neck. "People are talking nonsense. They're bored and grasping at gossip. Pay them no mind, babe."

Marlene sighed heavily. "I just want this all behind us. Maybe we should move the wedding somewhere else, get away from all the drama."

My heart sank, though I understood Marlene's frustration. All the work Aunt Meg and I had done to make this wedding perfect, and now here they were debating whether to continue. It was deeply disheartening.

He nodded slowly. "I have a buddy in Fredericksburg who owes me a favor. I bet he could get us a new venue fast!" His eyes jumped with excitement and my nerves went into high gear. This could not be happening. I busied myself restocking crackers, anxiously eaves-dropping. What if the wedding didn't happen here after all?

The bridesmaid who'd been bawling before Marlene came in stood and poured herself another very full glass of wine. "It wouldn't be that hard. I bet you could get the caterer to do the food still. It's not like Fredericksburg is that far away."

Clearly, no one realized the caterer was standing in the same room. Or that she had very important ties to Primrose House.

I cleared my throat. It was time to step in.

"Marlene, I know this whole murder situation has put a damper on your plans. But Primrose House is still your dream venue. I remember you telling me in an email that you'd always dreamed of having your wedding here as a girl. It's a real shame that this has happened, but you don't want to settle for good enough. You want to have your dream wedding. Please, I beg you, just give the police another day or two to figure this thing out. We'll keep working our hardest to make your dream wedding come true. You'll see, it'll all work out. Just have a little faith." I wish I believed it. But right now, it felt like everything about this wedding was coming off the rails.

Marlene sniffled, dabbing at her mascara-smudged eyes with a tissue. The soft lampshade lighting illuminated her distressed face. She nodded then, some of the tension leaving her shoulders.

"You're right. This is my dream, I can't give it up. It's got to be here, Derek. I can't change my mind now. Whoever doesn't like it can just kiss my backside." There was fight in her voice suddenly and I took it as a good sign.

"Yes, Marlene! We'll paint the town *and* the front porch!" her bridesmaid said and knocked back the rest of her wine. The fervor of it made me nervous about our poor alcohol supply. We might have to restock the cabinets after this little happy hour got through with.

"I'm just saying, Marlene, if you want to move this thing, I can make it happen. We don't need people saying bad things about us. I could move this wedding with a snap of my fingers! Anything for my angel bride," Derek said loudly, then leaned over and gave her a big smack of a kiss.

Oh, Derek. I willed him to go back to wherever he was staying and give us some peace.

Things settled down after that and I used the lull to clean up used plates and cups. Walking into the empty kitchen, I set the plates in the sink and let out a deep sigh and stretched my neck. The kitchen work alone had been enough to exhaust me, but with the murder and all the hubbub around it, I was feeling ready for bed even though the sun was still up. What I needed was a little fresh air.

I went through the kitchen door and out to the backyard. The evening was still warm and heat soaked into my shoulders. I closed my eyes for a moment, letting the warmth fill me. Between the body I'd found, the work for the wedding and happy hour, and all the catching up I'd done, I was absolutely beat. The work felt good, though. I was happy to be helping my aunt who'd done so much for my brother and me over the years. Opening my eyes, I strolled, absentmindedly walking along the path at the side of the house toward where I'd found Trisha's body earlier. I took a moment to admire Aunt Meg's flower beds near the window. Gladiolus in pinks, oranges, and ruby reds stood tall over a swath of shorter yellow snapdragons. I wondered where she got all the time and energy to do everything required of her at the B&B and still have time to grow show-stopping flower beds.

The tents had been raised during the day for the wedding, three big white canopies blocking out both sun and the possibility of rain. A rack of folding chairs stood to one side. I thought about calling Greg's assistant and ordering the equipment and cutlery we needed, but I wasn't ready to go back into work mode just yet. I figured it could wait until morning.

I thought about all the guests who were staying with us. Any of them could have killed Trisha. The ring and the fight made Marlene a very obvious suspect, but that didn't mean someone else who was staying here couldn't have murdered her. I hoped for Marlene's sake that the police knew more than I did. Because right at that moment, it looked like Marlene was guilty.

I drifted through the grass, thinking. The tire marks from Trisha's truck were still visible on the right side of where the tents stood. They were deep enough to see, but probably not deep enough to cause any overly inebriated guests to fall. I hadn't seen the police processing the scene, but I imagined they'd been all over the place looking for clues. Still, I couldn't help but scan the ground around the tire tracks, hoping to find something that might provide answers. Surely if the ground was wet enough to create tire tracks it was wet enough for footprints as well. Someone must have left Trisha's body in the yard. I doubted she drove herself over here. Unless she was meeting Marlene about something. But why would they be meeting out here in a rain storm? And if Marlene demanded she not be present, why would she later meet up with her?

I supposed if Marlene meant to kill her, she might have lured her over. But why here? Why in such a public spot? And one that would be certain to have a negative effect on Marlene's wedding? No, the idea that Marlene would have done this was almost impossible for me to believe. There had to be another explanation.

I recognized my slip-and-slide clog marks from the morning near the tire tracks. Those were obvious enough. I crouched down in the grass and stared at the marks for a moment, willing my eyes to see something, anything. But it was a big muddy mess.

Someone shouting at me from the front porch interrupted my thoughts. "Abby! Yoo hoo!"

CHAPTER TWELVE

I hightailed it to the front porch, hoping whoever was calling me wasn't looking for me with trouble. I rolled my shoulders as I walked back to the house, deciding to take the side path around to the front rather than go back inside. Who knew what fresh trouble brewed with the guests and their drinks? As I came around the front, I saw Cassie and Aunt Meg on the porch and smiled with relief.

"Abby! There you are!" Cassie said when she saw me. "We went looking for you. Go get a glass of wine and have a seat." They both smiled at me and I couldn't think of anything I'd like more. I headed into the kitchen for a glass of wine and came back out to sit on a rocker next to Aunt Meg.

"Sorry I ditched you in there for the happy hour, honey. A guest wanted my help booking a tour for tomorrow and it took longer than I expected it. Woo! These tourists sure are picky!"

"Don't worry about it," I told her. "I can do that kind of event in my sleep." It was best not to even mention the conversations I'd been a part of only a few minutes before. For now, the storm had blown over and I didn't want to worry Aunt Meg for no reason. She already had enough to stress about.

"Thanks so much for that happy hour, honey. You did a marvelous job. The guests were in a great mood when I checked on them," she said and patted my leg.

"You know I'm happy to help. But I'm just glad I was here. What would you have done otherwise?"

"Probably ordered a pile of takeout from Anna's," she replied with a cackle. "I'm glad you're here too. Wish it was for good. But I know you've got to do what's right for you, live your own life."

It yanked at my heart. I hated the idea that I was making her suffer. She'd cared so well for my brother and me over the years. And it made me feel bad that I'd abandoned her for a fancy life in California. Thankfully, Cassie changed the subject at that moment, regaling us with a hilarious story about someone who'd come into her shop that morning looking for a stuffed raccoon for their game room. It was enough to pull me out of my painful thoughts.

I sighed contentedly, settling into the rocking chair. It was good to take a moment and chat with Aunt Meg and Cassie. With everything swirling around Trisha's murder, I hadn't had a chance to catch up properly. We fell into easy conversation, reminiscing about our childhood adventures around the B&B. I could almost pretend it was just a normal night, laughing with family on the porch, and not think about all the work ahead of me.

After a while, the familiar rattling of the Connollys' old green Volkswagen van coming up the driveway pulled us back to the present. I sat up straighter, happy to see our long-time neighbors stopping by for a visit. A moment later Mark and Sheila Connolly climbed out and headed toward us, him carrying a large box.

Mark and Sheila had owned a vineyard to the west of us, *Wild Hare Winery*, longer than I could remember. They were a sweet couple who'd brought gifts over often when I was young—cookies or chocolates for my brother Devon and me, wine for Aunt Meg and Uncle Nolan. I always loved it when they stopped by, and it filled me with joy to see them coming up the porch in the late evening light.

"We heard you were back in town and had to come see for ourselves! It's so good to see you, girl!" Sheila was tiny and had the same firecracker energy that Aunt Meg possessed. I stood, and she gave me a powerful hug. Her hair had greyed considerably since I'd seen her last, and there were laugh lines around her eyes, but she was as fiery as ever.

Mark was a gigantic bear of a man with a long shaggy gray beard and a gruff smoker's voice. He'd invariably dressed in Grateful Dead t-shirts and jeans for the entire time I'd known him, and tonight was no different. He held the box out to Aunt Meg. "We brought y'all some of our new Riesling to try. Good to see ya, Abby!"

Aunt Meg took the box with a thanks and headed inside with it, coming back out a moment later with a freshly open bottle and two more glasses. "Have a seat," she told them and handed them each a glass of wine.

Sheila's face grew sad. "We heard about what happened to Trisha. How horrible." She turned to her husband. "You should tell them what you saw last night, baby," Sheila told Mark as she brushed his burly arm. Mark blushed at the endearment and took a drink before clearing his throat.

"I was out back having a last smoke," he cleared his throat again and glanced at Sheila out of the corner of his eye. She frowned at him and he shrugged and continued. "And it started pouring, one of those big ol' storms from out of nowhere. And then I saw a truck come up the road. I remember thinking about how that truck looked like it was gonna get stuck in the ditch 'cause it hopped over the yard over there. I watched for a while, wondering if I'd need to go get help because it just stayed put for the longest time. But then the lights went out and about five minutes later I saw another set of lights on the road light up and a sedan type car take off up toward town. It was odd, you know? Almost like that car'd been parked there and had just started up and gone after the truck arrived."

"About what time was this?" I asked.

Mark shrugged. "After midnight, but before two. I know I went to bed a little before two."

"Could it have been a guest returning?" Cassie asked Aunt Meg.

She frowned and shook her head. "It's possible, but I sincerely doubt it. There is a chime on the front door that sounds in my bedroom if the door is opened. I didn't hear anything," she replied and then turned to me. "Did you hear anything, Abby?"

"No, nothing. This seems like something the sheriff would want to know. Cassie, could you tell Ty?"

She nodded and pulled out her phone, sending a quick text. "Sure, that's a good idea. I thought he might come over with me tonight and meet you, but he was too busy, what with the murder and all. Maybe now you'll get a chance to meet him."

"No doubt. I wonder what they've found so far."

Cassie looked up from her phone a moment later. "Ty just texted back. He and the sheriff are going to come by to talk to Mark and look around. Check for any evidence from that other vehicle."

I nodded, feeling a glimmer of hope. "Any clues about that mystery car could really help."

Aunt Meg frowned. "But if it was raining hard, like Mark said, would there be any useful evidence left behind at this point?"

"There still could be traces they can test for," Cassie replied. "Fiber, mud patterns, anything distinctive. Especially if the car was on the side of the road."

Just then, flashing police lights appeared down the driveway as Ty arrived in his cruiser, followed by a dark sedan that must have been the sheriff's.

Mark stood, draining his wineglass. "Well, guess that's my cue." He ambled off to meet the officers.

After a few minutes of the men talking in the parking lot, Ty broke away from the other officers and headed over to us on the porch.

Cassie jumped up excitedly and pulled Ty in for a quick hug.

"Abby, this is Ty Clayburn. Ty, this is my best friend, Abby." She beamed at him and I was giddy for her. They made the cutest couple.

Ty tipped his hat politely. "Pleasure to meet you, Abby. I wish it was under better circumstances."

"Likewise," I replied.

"I'm so sorry, I can't stay to chat," Ty said with a glance toward the road. "We've got to process the scene for any traces of that mystery vehicle."

He gave Cassie a swift kiss on the cheek. "I'll call you later, babe. Nice seeing y'all."

With that, Ty hurried off to rejoin the deputies, who were now walking toward the main road.

As he headed off, Sheila sighed heavily. "What is this world coming to? A murder in our little town." She shivered despite the warm night.

Aunt Meg shook her head and squeezed Sheila's hand. "I just hope it doesn't interfere with the wedding. All this work and planning, and if it doesn't happen, oh!" She closed her eyes, and it pained me to see the worry on her face. I glanced at Cassie, who had the same expression.

"I know the sheriff and Ty are doing a fabulous job," I began, twirling my wineglass in my hands. "But maybe we should start looking into the murder ourselves? See if there's anything we can learn that the police might not."

Aunt Meg frowned, but Cassie's eyes shot up. "Yeah, I bet we could find out all kinds of things just snooping around here. People in town will talk your ear off, if you let them. But I doubt they'd be so open with the police."

"I really don't want y'all bothering the guests."

An excited buzz took over me. "We wouldn't bother anybody! Just keep eyes and ears open, right, Cass?"

Cassie nodded with an excitement that worried me a little. But I pressed on. "Just this evening, I overheard Marlene and her mother in the kitchen talking about how it was her ring they found under Trisha's body. They didn't even realize I was there. I bet between us all, we could pick up some pretty good clues that the police might otherwise miss."

Aunt Meg looked skeptical, but then she shrugged. "I guess it couldn't hurt. Especially if it means we figure out what's happened before the wedding. Just don't go bothering my guests, y'all hear?"

Cassie and I smiled at each other and nodded. Was this really happening? I loved my true crime shows, but this felt much more serious suddenly. I immediately started to rethink it, but Cassie clearly had no such reservations.

"I can keep my ears out about who Trisha was sleeping with. The way people talk in this town, it shouldn't take long to find something out."

I nodded excitedly, the worry from a few seconds earlier dissipating at Cassie's plans. "I can see what I can find out from the B&B. Maybe dig in with Marlene a little and try to clear her name. I'm more and more certain it wasn't her. It doesn't add up. If anything, she's being framed."

Aunt Meg joined in. "I'll ask Maria tomorrow if she noticed anything while tidying rooms."

It made me giddy that Aunt Meg was getting in on the plans. "I just wish we had a way to get into Trisha's place. I bet there's all sorts of evidence."

"I'm sure the police already went through it with a fine-tooth comb."

We all nodded solemnly. "Cassie, I'd normally hate to suggest this, but maybe you could pry a bit with Ty? See if he'll let you know what they've found out so far?"

"I could try!"

"I'll talk to Trisha's partner, Greg, tomorrow, too, if I see him around. He seemed strange this morning. I saw him arguing with Janine." I shrugged.

Our impromptu investigation plans gave me hope. For the first time since finding Trisha's body, I felt a sense of purpose. We all seemed committed to getting justice for Trisha and clearing Marlene's name before the wedding.

As we said goodnight, I knew we'd have to be cautious in seeking the truth. But with Cassie's connections, Aunt Meg's intuition, and my determination, I believed we could unravel this mystery.

Chapter Thirteen

Early the next morning, I drove over to the store to buy ingredients I would need for the reception dinner. It wasn't entirely clear that the wedding would actually take place, but if I didn't start prepping, I would be in deep trouble come Saturday.

After I arrived back at *Primrose House,* I quickly put my purchases away and pulled my apron over my head. I would need several more trips to the store over the next couple of days, but I wanted to start the prep work early and do what I could without overwhelming the fridge space too soon. I'd stopped by Mark and Sheila's place on the way home to borrow three large ice chests for extra space, but I knew that before long our little kitchen would be full to the brim with serving platters and containers full of wedding food.

I got to work chopping vegetables for a base sauce I would serve with the steaks but before I even made it through the pile of celery, Cassie came bursting through the back door.

I steadied my knife in case she tried to bear hug me again and raised my eyebrows when I realized how out of breath she was. "Abby, you busy?"

I looked down at my cutting board and back at her.

"Okay, obviously you are. But I have something really important for us to do."

"Okay..."

"Last night Ty stayed over," she blushed, and I graciously ignored it. "And he had Trisha's keys with him, and I got a copy."

"What?"

"The keys to Trisha's apartment! I have them. I thought we could go look around," she whispered.

I put the knife down and came around the counter next to her. "Are you serious?" I whispered back. "How'd you get them?"

"He just left them on the desk. And I remembered what you said about wishing we could check her place out. So I got the keys, and I made a copy."

"How do you know they're Trisha's?"

She shrugged. "I asked him what they were, and he told me."

"How did you make a copy without him finding out?"

"I have a key copying machine at the store. I bought one a while ago. They really aren't very expensive and it gets people into the shop."

I raised my eyebrows, and she continued. "So anyway, he was in the shower and I just... well, I just borrowed them for a few minutes and went over to the shop and copied them."

"Do you have her car key, too?"

"Probably. There were a bunch of keys on the ring. Probably shop keys or something like that, maybe for mail? I don't know. I copied them all." She pulled a key ring out of her purse and jingled it in front of my face.

I glanced at the countertops covered with prep work for the wedding and bit my lip. "How far away does she live?"

"Maybe ten minutes from here."

I grabbed a large Tupperware and began scooping my half chopped celery in. "Okay, but it has to be fast. I've got a lot to do today."

Cassie grinned and smiled. "I can help you when we're done if you need me to." She made a little yip of excitement as I peeled my apron off and hung it in the pantry. "I feel like Nancy Drew."

I smiled back and followed her out the kitchen door and around to her truck, ducking my head as I did and hoping not to run into Aunt Meg. It was bad enough I was shirking my culinary duties, but I didn't want her asking questions. Knowing I was about to break the law and enter a dead woman's home gave me the jitters. But having to fess up to my aunt would have stopped me in my tracks, and I was truly eager to see what secrets Trisha's place held. I crossed my fingers as we ran through the parking lot and breathed a sigh of relief as we got to Cassie's truck and I slid in.

I was nervous as we headed down the highway toward the far side of town where Trisha lived and I fidgeted. "You sure this is a good idea?" I asked her. Her face was as determined as I'd ever seen it, and I already knew her answer. "Aren't you worried about getting into trouble? What if somebody sees us? What if Ty finds out?"

"He's at the office. He isn't going to find out. This is important, right? I mean, if we don't get Marlene cleared, the wedding might not happen. And if the wedding doesn't happen, Aunt Meg's business might be in jeopardy. From where I'm sitting, I don't think we have any choice."

"What if we leave evidence behind?" I gasped suddenly. "We should have gloves. Do you have any gloves?"

She frowned and popped the glove box open. "I think there are some gardening gloves in there. Take a look." Shockingly, she was right, and I pulled out two pairs of hot pink gardening gloves.

"We should probably wait to put these on until we get inside," I told her and from the nervousness and absolute absurdity of the situation, I burst out laughing. Cassie did the same, and we had ourselves a good long laugh as we sped through town.

Cassie pulled into the parking lot of the run-down apartment complex a few minutes later and we cautiously left the truck, watching for neighbors as we headed up the path to 4-B. The coast seemed clear, but there were an awful lot of windows around. I was going to need some alka-seltzer after this little adventure. No doubt about it.

As we reached the door, I handed her a pair of the gloves. She slid them on and then pulled out the keys and tried a few before getting the right one and pushing the door open. We entered quickly and closed the door behind us.

The place was a disaster. I don't know if the police had trashed Trisha's house or if she'd created all the chaos herself, but the disorder gave me the heebie-jeebies. I shuddered at the sink piled with moldy dishes and pulled on my pair of gloves.

"Maybe start in the bedroom? I bet that's where the good stuff is," Cassie said, eyeing the Everest sized pile of dirty laundry on the living room floor.

We crept down the hallway, trying to be careful not to leave any evidence of our visit. The bed was a tangled mess of sheets, and I quickly noticed a man's button-down shirt balled up in the corner. We exchanged a look. This could be evidence of the rumored affair, which could very well have been connected to her death.

I stooped and straightened out the shirt. It was light blue with unusual gold buttons that had tiny engraved stars on them. Near the neck of the shirt, a dark lipstick stain stood out. I frowned and made a mental note to check Trisha's lipsticks to see if I could find a match.

Next, I stood with my hands on my hips and looked at the bed. I hesitated before I grabbed the sheets. It felt wrong somehow to be messing with a crime scene like this. But the police had already been through, right? Surely they'd gotten what they'd come for. Pulling the comforter off the bed, I shook it, then placed it on a chair. I wasn't sure what I was looking for, but if this really was about an affair, it seemed reasonable that there might be some evidence in the bed. I grabbed the top sheet to shake it out, but stopped when I saw a glint of gold.

Bending down, I picked up a small earring that looked like a teardrop. It was gold that ended with a splash of a red color at the bottom. The latch was delicate, and I puzzled over it a moment before putting it on the dresser and continuing with my search of the bed.

Cassie scouted around for clues in the closet while I looked through the dresser drawers and nightstands for anything that might explain why someone would want Trisha dead. In one drawer, under a pile of papers and junk half stuck underneath the corner, I found an old envelope with Trisha's name printed across the front. My heart skipped a beat as I tugged it out, unfolded it, and began to read.

"Cassie! Look at this!" I smoothed the crumpled paper and held it up to the light as Cassie bent over my shoulder.

Trisha, if you do not stop sticking your nose into things that aren't yours, you'll be sorry. Drop this thing or you are dead!

"Whoa. That seems important. I wonder why Ty didn't take it?"

"It was all crumpled up and stuck in the very back. He probably didn't see it through all the rest of this junk." I poked at the papers, wrappers, rubber bands, and a thousand pens that overflowed out of the drawer.

As I did, another crumpled paper caught my attention, and I pulled it out, too. It was a spreadsheet of finance information from Wildflower Rentals. She was part owner, so having a financial statement from the company didn't surprise me. But something about it gave me pause. I pulled out my phone and snapped a quick picture.

"The note isn't signed. Who do you think it's from?"

Cassie straightened up and shrugged. "No clue. Let's see what else there is. Maybe we'll find something that will help us figure it out."

"Do you think we should take it with us? Or leave it here?"

"Isn't it a crime to take something from a crime scene?"

No doubt. "Well, we can't just keep it to ourselves. Should we tell Ty about it?" I bit my lip. This was getting tricky fast. I hadn't actually thought about the possibility of finding something important.

Just at that moment, someone knocked on the door and we both froze. "Shoot!" Cassie said under her breath. "What do we do?"

"Hello? I know someone's in there!"

"Let's say we're here to clean," I whispered. Cassie's eyes lit up, and she nodded. I grabbed a half filled garbage bag from the kitchen and moved to the door. "Good morning," I said as I swung it open, revealing an elderly woman with frizzy whisps of hair and massive glasses.

"Hey, what y'all doin' in there? This is where that dead woman lived."

I nodded. "Yes, ma'am. We're the cleaning people. The police sent us over."

She frowned but didn't question it. "Oh, well. Alright then. I just wanted to make sure it wasn't that hussie who was over here making all the racket the other night."

Cassie and I glanced at each other. "I'm sorry?" I asked.

"That one who was over the other night yellin' up a storm! Them two women were making all sorts of noise. I thought they'd never shut up!"

"Did you hear what they were fighting about?"

"Lord, I have no idea. I'm deaf as a post. They must've really been at it for me to hear," she laughed and stepped back. "Well, I'll let you get back to your work, then." She craned her head around to look inside and made a face. "I don't envy y'all. Best of luck."

I stuck my head out the door and glanced around the apartment grounds quickly before shutting the door. "That was way too close for comfort, Cass. We gotta get out of here."

She nodded. "Take a picture of that note before we leave. Better than nothing."

I did what she said quickly and then we put things back as close as we could to how they were when we'd arrived. Throwing one last glance around as we left, my heart jumped in my throat. I wished we would have had more time, but I knew we were pressing our luck as it was. The last thing I wanted was to get Cassie in trouble.

CHAPTER FOURTEEN

As Cassie drove us back to the B&B, we could hardly contain our excitement over the potential evidence we'd uncovered.

"That note proves someone threatened Trisha before she died," I said.

Cassie nodded enthusiastically. "It didn't seem like something that would have come from Marlene."

"And the shirt was interesting," she added. "Do you think it belongs to the man she was seeing?"

"Could be. Or it could be one from an old beau. Who knows?"

We speculated about what it all meant during the short drive back to *Primrose House*. Everything we found seemed important, but I didn't know why. At least not yet.

Cassie dropped me off at the side of the B&B. She told me she would try to find out more about Trisha's love life, and I promised to find out more about Trisha and Greg's business. After a quick hug, I rushed back through the side yard, hoping nobody had missed me in my absence. I poked my head into the kitchen and, finding it empty, I sighed with relief and slipped inside. Grabbing my apron, I turned back to the prep work I'd put aside for our little scouting mission and was soon in the zone with my chores.

My head spun nearly as fast as my knife chopping vegetables. But I forced myself to focus on the wedding prep, determined to do Marlene proud. The clues Cassie and I found had energized me. It felt like there might be a way for us to get Marlene off the hook. I just needed to figure out what it all meant.

The scent of garlic and onions perfumed the air as I chopped vegetables for the wedding feast. I was so focused on the rhythmic thunk of the knife that I didn't hear Maria come in.

"Need any help?" she asked, making me jump. I turned to see the petite young woman gazing around at the overflowing countertops.

"That would be amazing. There's so much to do before Saturday," I said. Maria nodded somberly, her dark ponytail swaying.

"It's terrible about that woman... Trisha, was it? Being killed right here." She tied on an apron and started tidying the mess I'd made. I handed her a cutting board and knife and pointed to the onions. "If you could dice those up, that would be great."

She nodded and started chopping. "I heard they think it may be one of the guests. Is this true?"

I frowned. "It seems that way. The bride-to-be, if you can believe it. Personally, I have other theories." I lowered my voice and glanced at her. Something about her made me want to open up. Plus, I thought it might be a good idea to enlist her help if she was willing. "I probably shouldn't say anything, but my friend Cassie and I have been doing a little sleuthing about the murder on the side."

Maria's brown eyes went wide. "Like detectives? Do you have clues?" She leaned forward eagerly.

"We may be onto something promising," I confessed. I looked around, unsure of who might be listening. "But we have to be very discreet about it. I'll tell you more later."

"I would love to help with clues! I can keep my eyes and ears open around here without anyone noticing, too," Maria pledged with a grin. "One of the upsides of what we do, nobody ever seems to notice us. Am I right?"

I smiled and nodded, feeling a rush of gratitude for her willingness to help. With Maria's help, we might just solve this mystery before the wedding got canceled. After a few moments of companionable work, I left Maria to watch my sauce and fished in my pocket for the card Greg had given me the morning before. I needed to get supplies ordered, or we would be in trouble. Not only that, but the financial printout was at the back of my mind. Maybe Stacy would want to talk about more than just rentals.

"Good morning, Wildflower Rentals," a sugary voice with a thick country accent said.

"Hi, is this Stacy?"

"Yes, Ma'am."

"Hi my name is Abby Hirsch. I'm working over at Primrose House for a wedding this weekend? I wanted to order some rentals from y'all, and Greg told me to call you and place an order."

"Oh, right! He told me to expect your call," her voice turned sullen. "You're the one who found Trisha, right?"

I cleared my throat, surprised at the question. I hadn't expected to talk about Trisha and it threw me off. "Yep. That was me."

"It must've been awful. Lord! I can't imagine!"

"It was." I sighed and sat down at the kitchen table. Seemed like she was hankering to talk and I might be on the phone for a while.

"Greg and Trisha were always arguing! It was awful. Totally toxic work environment, you know what I mean? I hate to say it, but it'll be much more pleasant now that she's gone. Not that I wanted her to die or anything! I just hated all the arguing!"

This was interesting. "What did they argue over?"

"Everything! But mostly money. They thought I couldn't hear because the door was closed, but let me tell you, those two were noisy as a restless mule in a tin barn. Yelled it up a blue streak just last week about insurance money or some such."

"Insurance money?"

"Yeah, Trisha said Greg was trying to pull something. She had a bunch of printouts and was waving them around. They went into the office and yelled at each other about it for a while."

I tapped my pen on my notepad, intrigued by Stacy's insider information but also feeling guilty hearing her speak ill of the dead. Not to mention I was itchy to get my order placed and move on with my day. Curiosity won out.

"I probably shouldn't pry... but did you have any sense what they were fighting about with the insurance money?" I asked. Stacy seemed eager to vent.

"Oh, who knows with those two! Something like, 'If you keep scraping money off the top, this business is going to fail! I'll turn you in, I swear to God!' And then he said, 'your attitude with clients is what's driving our business to fail! I'd be better off running this business by myself', that sort of thing. It went on and on like that for a while. Eventually I went to lunch, I was so sick of the noise. But that's how it was all the time when the two of them were in the office together. It's much more peaceful around here now."

I made a noncommittal noise and wondered whether I should press for more or steer us toward getting supplies ordered.

Sensing my hesitation, Stacy backtracked. "Sorry, I shouldn't speak so plainly. Trisha was a nice lady most of the time. It's a darn shame how it ended for her. And poor Greg too. What a mess. I don't know how he's going to do it all now that she's gone."

I decided it was best not to pry further into Greg and Trisha's disputes. There would be time for investigating later. Right now, I needed to focus on getting the supplies ordered for the wedding.

"Let's get that rental order completed," I said, steering the conversation to logistics.

I heard Stacy shuffling papers on the other end. "Okay, what all do you need? Greg said something about dishes?"

I glanced at my checklist, reading off items one by one. Stacy asked questions, confirming stock and pricing as we went, and I heard her typing furiously as she took my order.

"And we'll need champagne flutes for the toasts, probably about 150 of those," I said.

"No problem, I'll have them pull extra so you have spares," Stacy replied.

We agreed on Greg delivering everything at 10AM Friday morning, which made my heart flutter. Realizing how little time before the wedding I had did nothing for my nerves. But after finalizing the substantial order, and hanging up with Stacy, I felt relieved to have one major task accomplished.

As I went back to my prep work, my mind returned to Stacy's comments. Greg and Trisha's money issues nagged at me. Perhaps those rental records we'd found in Trisha's apartment could reveal clues about the tensions between them. But for right now, I forced myself to focus on the job at hand—pulling off a perfect wedding amidst murder and mayhem.

CHAPTER FIFTEEN

After another hour of prep work, Maria had to leave for the day. I was truly grateful for her help, especially with Trisha's murder occupying so much of my energy. As she headed out, I decided it was time for a break myself, and sank into one of the oak chairs at the antique table. I desperately needed some rest. My eyes landed on the plate of brownies leftover from the previous night's happy hour, and my mouth watered.

I got up and poured myself a glass of sweet tea from the fridge and took a long, refreshing sip. The hint of mint and sweetness soothed my nerves. Selecting a corner brownie, I leaned back and closed my eyes as the sugary goodness melted on my tongue.

Taking a deep breath, I tried to gather my spiraling thoughts. My conversation with Stacy troubled me, and I tried to put what she told me together with what Cassie and I had found at Trisha's earlier that morning. There was something there, and it nagged at me, but it wasn't coming. Maybe if I slept on it, I would get some clarity. The thought of a nap was a siren call I could not afford to heed, though. There were only two more days left to prep for this thing before the big day, and I had a mountain of work to do.

I'd just taken another bite of brownie when I heard boots on the creaky floorboards. I turned to see Sheriff Ryan Iverson's tall frame filling the doorway, his dark hair glinting in the sun filtering through the window.

"Sorry to interrupt your break, Ma'am," he said, his green eyes crinkling at the corners. "But I'm here for Marlene. Do you know where she might be?"

I nodded my head and tried not to look like a deer in headlights. I felt suddenly ready to puke up the brownie I'd just eaten. The irrational idea that he knew about Cassie and me breaking into Trisha's house ate away at me. "She and the bridesmaids went out on a winery tour this morning. They should be back around three."

He pushed a button on the radio that was attached to his shoulder. "She's not here. Should be back by three. Keep an eye on the parking lot for me, will you, Ty?"

"No problem, sir."

Sheriff Iverson eyed the brownie on my plate and then met my gaze once more. "Since I need to wait for her, would you mind if I took a few minutes of your time to go over a few follow-up questions with you about Trisha McBride's death?"

My pulse quickened as I nodded. "Please, have a seat. Can I get you something? Tea? Brownie?" I motioned to the spread on the table, hoping my voice sounded steadier than I felt.

"I'd appreciate that. Thanks." The sheriff sat down in the chair nearest me, the wood groaning under his muscular build. His knee accidentally brushed mine as I sat back down, sending a flurry of sparks through me. *Get it together, Abby!*

"I understand you aren't from here," he asked before taking a sip of tea.

"I'm from here. Just haven't been back in a while. I went to college in Austin, and I've been living in L.A. the last two years because I've been in culinary school. I came back this week to help Aunt Meg out with Marlene's wedding."

He took a bite of the brownie and I watched a spark of pure enjoyment move across his face. I smiled in response. Creating pleasure through food was the highlight of my work. He saw me watching him and smiled quickly before setting down his brownie and flipping open his notepad, suddenly all business.

"Take me back to the morning you found Trisha. Does anything stand out to you about the morning in particular, or what you saw you might not have recalled when we spoke before? I'm not trying to question your memory. I hope you understand, Ma'am. It's just that people forget little details all the time while they're in the immediate shock of the situation."

"You can call me Abby. You don't have to Ma'am me." I gave him a disarming smile, and he relaxed back in his chair and smiled back.

"Of course. Abby."

"No, I don't think I missed anything. She was still wearing the same clothes from the day before. I don't know if anyone mentioned that."

He nodded and snuck another bite of brownie, washing it down with the tea.

"What about unusual visitors on the property? I know some number of strangers is normal for a business such as your aunt's, but does anything stand out as unusual to you?"

I thought about the man who'd accused Marlene. The one who seemed so thrilled whenever things went poorly for her. Should I say something? But what was there to say, even? "I've only been here a couple of days, but no one really stands out to me as suspicious. Just the normal guests and staff, along with the rental company crew getting set up. The Connollys stop by and bring us wine often. And Janine lives down the street, so she's here a lot."

He nodded, jotting this down. "And no strange vehicles driving by or unknown people wandering around?"

"No, nothing like that."

"What about Marlene Lewis? Did you see her at all the morning you found Trisha? Before we arrived, I mean."

"No. As far as I know, I was the only one awake until I found the body."

He nodded. "And the fight she had with the deceased... would you characterize it as serious, or was it more like a small spat?"

I wish I knew. "Honestly, I don't know either of them, but it's pretty clear they had a history. From my angle as a sort of outsider, the fight didn't seem that serious. But I could be missing something. There's always a story behind the story, you know what I mean?"

He nodded, and I took a sip of my tea, grateful for the coldness of it. My cheeks were burning with his questions and close proximity. What was wrong with me? I felt the need to remove the pressure of his scrutiny suddenly, give myself a breather.

"So what brought you to Sugar Creek, anyway? You're obviously not from around here originally," I asked him suddenly, not having any idea where the question came from. Something about the man captivated me, and I wanted to know more about him.

He leaned back in his chair and nodded. "You're right, I'm not. I actually just moved here a few months ago from Dallas."

"Wow, that must have been quite the change of pace," I said.

"You could say that," he chuckled. "Dallas kept me real busy. I'd worked with Ty in Dallas for a few years before he moved down here. Once he moved, he kept talking about how nice it was. Eventually, I followed. We had a lot of murder cases up there in Dallas, as you can imagine. And it wears on you after a while, you know? I left for a smaller town and I'd hoped to leave all that behind. "

I nodded sympathetically.

He continued, "But people are people everywhere you go, I suppose. No getting away from it. I'm sorry that it had to happen here during such a big event for y'all. I know how hard that must be."

"It's difficult, that's for sure. My biggest concern is that the wedding won't happen at all. Of course, I feel awful for the woman who died, and I want to have the person who did it arrested, but we've worked so hard around here to make this wedding happen. It'd be a shame if it didn't work out." I was fishing, and he knew it.

He sipped the last of his tea. "I wish I could give you good news on that front. But with an open investigation like this, there's no telling how things will end up. We're looking in multiple directions at the moment, but we feel strongly that there's a connection between Ms. McBride's murder and the B&B."

I cleared my throat. "I heard through the grapevine that Trisha might have been sleeping with a married man. Do you know anything about that? Is it something y'all are investigating?" I felt a blush creep up at my question, feeling suddenly silly for grilling a police officer.

"It's something we're looking into. Look, I know y'all are worried about Marlene and the wedding. I get that. But I promise you we're doing our job the best we can. I appreciate you sharing that with me, though. If there's anything else you come across, I'd like to hear about it."

My heart skipped a beat thinking about the things we'd found at Trisha's house that morning. But my guess was that if I admitted to breaking into her place, I would be in a world of trouble. Maybe even get myself arrested. And that wouldn't do anybody any good. I took a deep breath and gave him a big smile. "Will do, Sheriff Iverson."

"You can call me Ryan. You don't have to sheriff me." His smile was full of fun and I returned it as he stood and tucked the chair back beneath the table. I stood as well and took our empty dishes to the sink, relieved that his questions hadn't turned in my direction.

I felt suddenly shy as we stared at each other in silence in the cozy kitchen.

"Well, I should go and let you get back to your day," Ryan said finally, his eyes lingering on me still. "Thank you for the hospitality. The brownie was delicious. And thank you for being open with me. It really will help the investigation."

I fought the guilt about Trisha's apartment as I walked him through the house to the front door. The sitting room was empty of guests and tidy. I wondered where Aunt Meg was, suddenly aware that I hadn't seen her since breakfast. I made a mental note to go look for her after Ryan left.

Ryan turned to me with his hand on the front door. "I know this whole situation is a lot to deal with. But if you ever need to talk more —about anything—please call me. Any time." He handed me his card, his fingers grazing mine.

My heart fluttered as I met his earnest gaze. "I will. And please let me know if there's anything I can do to help. I want to see justice for Trisha as much as you."

Ryan nodded, then tipped his hat and started down the steps. But just as he did, the rumble of an engine approached, and a hulking white party bus emblazoned with "Two-Step Through Texas Tours" in neon green pulled up in front of the porch.

CHAPTER SIXTEEN

The doors of the bus swung open with a hydraulic hiss, and distressed B&B guests began pouring out into the afternoon sun.

This did not look good.

Marlene and her four bridesmaids were the first ones off the bus. They looked sickly and miserable, their faces pale and beaded with sweat. I noticed ugly purple-red stains down the front of several of their dresses. As they came down from the bus, I saw Ty heading up from the parking lot where he'd been waiting next to the police cruiser. He seemed stiff and ready to pounce, and it put me on edge even more as I watched the wedding party climb the steps to the B&B.

"Ugghh, I feel like I'm going to puke again," one bridesmaid groaned, leaning against the porch railing for support as she made her way up the steps.

The rest of the bus passengers filed out behind them, looking irritated. I overheard grumbles about how the tour got cut short and how they deserved a refund.

Last off the bus was the man who'd been so vocal the morning before about Marlene and Trisha's fight. The same one who'd so enjoyed the bridesmaids' meltdown at the happy hour. He had a subtle smirk tugging at his lips as he surveyed the unhappy wedding party.

There was something suspicious about him and I frowned and put my hands on my hips as I watched him bound up the steps with a smile on his face, swinging a big travel backpack behind him.

What was that man's deal?

"This is a disaster!" Marlene cried, fanning herself as tears sprang to her eyes. "Our vineyard tour was ruined! And look at my dress! Why is everything going wrong for me?" The others murmured agreement and headed toward the door, dabbing ineffectually at the wine stains.

But before Marlene could move inside, Ryan stepped in front of her. "I'm very sorry, Ma'am. But I'm going to have to take you with us to the station."

Marlene turned white as a sheet.

"Excuse me?"

"We have reason to believe you may have been involved in the murder of Trisha McBride. You are being arrested, Ma'am."

Marlene fell to the ground and wailed. It was not pretty.

Ryan motioned to Ty, who came around with handcuffs. I had absolutely no envy for the man. Marlene flailed and cried and Ty looked to Ryan for some guidance.

"How can you do this to me? You can't possibly believe I killed her! Why would I do that?"

Ryan stepped forward and bent to put handcuffs on her, but she flailed even more furiously. I felt the crowd around us growing in size and intensity. I hoped it wouldn't turn into a brawl. The way the sick bridesmaids were looking, I thought anything was possible.

"Please, Ma'am. Don't do this. I don't want to have to drag you out of here."

Marlene bawled another minute on the porch, but as he started to reach for her arm, she stood. "Okay, okay! But I didn't kill her! You have to believe me!" Her eyes scanned the crowd wildly and then landed on me. "Abby, you know I couldn't have done this! You've got to help me. Don't let them ruin my wedding." She pulled herself together and, with more strength in her voice, turned back to Ryan. "Do you have any idea how much I have to do today? There are only three more days until my wedding! You can't do this! It'll ruin everything!" Just as he got one handcuff on her wrist, she leaned over the porch rail and puked.

A collective cringe passed through the onlookers. Poor Marlene. She was not having a good day.

Ryan waited until her sickness passed and one of her bridesmaids handed her a handkerchief before putting the other handcuff on her.

"I can't believe you would do something like this to me right now! You are heartless, Sheriff! Absolutely heartless!"

He nodded and angled her toward the cruiser. "I know, Ma'am. But you are under arrest for murder. You have the right to remain silent..." His litany mixed with Marlene's wails as the two made their way through the parking lot.

Finally, they put her in the car and Ryan and Ty got in and drove off. The crowd began to disperse and only then I noticed Aunt Meg standing close to me, hugging her body.

"What a sad thing," she said. "This wedding seems to be cursed, Abby. If Marlene's in jail, we'll definitely have to cancel it." She frowned and headed inside, and my stomach sank. What could I possibly do? I knew Marlene was innocent. I just knew it! But how could I prove that to the sheriff and get her out of jail in time to save this wedding?

I noticed the tour bus manager, who was grabbing bags from the underside storage. Realizing it was Ed Morton, who I'd known in high school, I decided to talk to him about what had happened on the tour. "Hey, Ed, long time no see! How are things?"

"Abby Hirsch! Good to see ya! I heard you'd come back to town. Nice to have you back."

I smiled and helped him with move the rest of the bags to the porch. "I'm just here for a visit. For now anyway. What went wrong out there today?"

Ed shook his head. "I've never seen anything like it. About halfway through, the entire wedding party started complaining of stomach cramps and puking. We had to cut the vineyard tour short."

"That's awful," I replied. "But the other guests were okay?"

"Yep, perfectly fine," Ed confirmed. "It was just those bridesmaids and the bride who got sick. Such a shame."

"Hopefully they didn't do too much damage to your bus." Poor Ed. I couldn't imagine how painful the ride home must have been.

He gave me an affable smile. "It's no big deal. Trust me, when I decided to drive drunk tourists around for a living, I knew what I was getting into. It happens. At least they usually feel obligated to leave a big tip." He laughed and shrugged, shutting the hatch of the bus. "Good luck to y'all over here. I think you're going to need it. Especially this afternoon."

I waved him off and then headed in to find Aunt Meg. I wanted to know more about the mystery man who'd seemed so happy getting off the bus.

She was coming down the stairs with a full trash bag, a sour look on her face. "Can you believe the rotten luck? Those poor girls are sick as dogs. I hope Marlene is being treated properly over at the station." She shook her head.

I followed her into the kitchen and waited while she tossed the bag out in the dumpster outside the door.

"It's strange that it was just the wedding party that got sick, don't you think?"

"Sure is. Could have been food poisoning, I suppose. Seems those girls are tied at the hip most of the time."

I nodded, but I wasn't convinced. Something felt off to me.

"What do you know about that guest who told the sheriff about Marlene and Trisha fighting? I keep seeing him pop up in strange circumstances."

She frowned, thinking. "Was it the Californian? The one who's celebrating his anniversary with his wife?"

I shook my head. "No, the one who's here on his own. He's a little on the short side. Balding."

Her eyes lit up, and she moved to the front of the house. I followed, and she pulled out the guest book. "I know who you're talking about." She fingered the book and flipped a page. "Okay, Donald Watts. I'm almost certain that's the man you're thinking of."

"Is he here for the wedding?"

"I don't think so. I haven't seen him interacting with anyone in the wedding party. And I remember overhearing when he checked in with Maria that he's on vacation by himself, something about a sabbatical from work."

"Do you know offhand where he's from?"

Aunt Meg frowned thoughtfully and looked back down at the book. "Let's see... ah, from Plano, Texas."

"Isn't Plano where Marlene lives?" I asked.

Aunt Meg nodded and looked at me quizzically.

"Seems like quite a coincidence. Are you sure he doesn't know her?"

Aunt Meg shook her head and frowned. "I don't know for certain, but I got the impression that he didn't know anybody here."

Maybe it *was* just a lot of coincidences. But I was going to keep a sharper eye on him. And I thought I might ask Maria to keep her eyes open when she cleaned his room the next morning. I wanted to know what he was up to, if only to ease my mind.

CHAPTER SEVENTEEN

Going back to the kitchen, I leaned against the counter, absolutely drained. It was hard to wrap my head around the fact that I'd only been back in Sugar Creek for forty-eight hours. So much had happened in that time, starting with Trisha's murder the morning before and culminating in Marlene's arrest. It felt like a lifetime had passed since Cassie and I had snuck into Trisha's apartment, but it had only been a few hours since our foray into breaking and entering.

My mind flashed back to the threat and the printouts. I wish I knew what it meant. Pulling my phone out, I scrolled through the pictures we'd taken. I wondered if the person who had sent her the note was the same person who'd killed her. What had she done to deserve such a ferocious threat? Would Marlene have any reason to send her something like it? It seemed their fight was more of an out-in-the-open type of thing than a sending-unsigned-threatening-notes kind of thing. But I didn't know enough to be sure.

Sighing, I put away my phone, frustrated at not knowing enough to put it all together, and then pulled open the fridge and made a quick scan of what was inside. I'd already set out the usual happy hour food that Maria had prepped before leaving for the day, and I realized I was starving. I'd been so busy between wedding chores, sleuthing, talking to the sheriff, and settling arguments, that I'd barely eaten. My stomach rumbled as I moved cartons of half-ready wedding food around, but found little more than a head of lettuce and some chicken salad that I wasn't sure of. I wondered if Aunt Meg had eaten yet and thought I should probably make enough for both of us. She'd been as busy as me all day and I doubted she'd had much to eat either.

Luckily, at just that moment, Cassie popped into the kitchen and saved me from the misery of a sad dinner.

"Lady! What do you say to some barbecue? We have a lot to discuss." The way she said it, I could tell she'd heard about Marlene's arrest.

I grinned and threw the chicken salad back in the fridge. "Sounds delicious! Let me go see what Aunt Meg is up to. She might want to come too."

I found Aunt Meg playing cards with a couple from North Carolina. I tried to convince her to come out with Cassie and me, but she'd declined, so I promised I'd bring her back a brisket sandwich before grabbing my purse and heading out to Cassie's waiting truck.

Lulu's was a quaint mom and pop place with a handful of tables and booths draped in red and white checkered tablecloths. Shelves along the weathered wooden walls displayed Lulu's collection of barbecue trophies and small town newspaper clippings. Rolls of paper towels sat clustered in the center of each table alongside squeeze bottles of tangy sauce. Old country music twanged in the background.

We ordered at the counter—brisket with baked beans and potato salad and a Dr. Pepper for me and pulled pork with coleslaw and sweet tea for Cassie—and then settled into a booth by the front window, far enough away from the few other diners that I felt comfortable talking about the sordid details of our amateur investigation.

Cassie looked over her shoulder and leaned in. "Ty told me they arrested Marlene! I tried my best to pry something out of him. Darn police officers are so goody two-shoes. Didn't get a thing, other than the fact that she was sick as a dog."

I nodded. "I guess they all got sick on a wine tour this afternoon. It was only the wedding party, though. Seems suspicious to me."

"You think someone poisoned them or something?"

I shrugged, thinking back to the smirking man. "I don't know. It's possible. I'm going to see what I can find out about one of the guests who keeps showing up whenever things get tough for Marlene. I don't know if he has any role to play, but he seems suspicious."

She nodded. "Good idea. Keep multiple lines of inquiry open. There's so much going on! It's hard to keep track of it all." She paused and looked around, then leaned in again. "So, what do you think? You think that note is from the killer?"

I raised my eyebrows and fiddled with the ketchup bottle. "Could be. But I'm interested in the romance angle too. You're right, there's so much going on, it's hard to make sense of it! The one thing I'm almost positive about, though, is that it wasn't Marlene. I wonder why they arrested her. They must know something more than we do. Surely it can't just be because of that ring."

Cassie nodded. "I went digging on Trisha through the grapevine this morning. She was indeed seeing someone over in Fredericksburg until recently, Joe Blackburn. They broke up about eight months ago. Before that she'd slept with Lyla Hornsby's husband, Rick, and that was a big hubbub around town. Old Doris at the post office gave me the lowdown. I guess the wife caught on and threatened her with a shotgun."

"Could that have been the person who sent the note?"

Her eyebrows raised. "I hadn't thought of that, but it's possible. Although that affair was a while back now, maybe over a year? Not sure why she'd keep that note for so long."

Our food came to our table then, two heaping piles of deliciousness delivered by a teenager I didn't recognize. I'd been gone from Sugar Creek for so long that I felt like I was an out-of-towner. It wasn't a feeling I enjoyed.

I squirted out Lulu's signature tangy barbecue sauce on the side of my plate and dipped a juicy piece of brisket in before popping it in my mouth. The taste was pure heaven. There was nothing quite like good Texas barbecue. I closed my eyes and savored it a moment before Cassie brought me back to reality.

"Anyway, I didn't learn much about the current man, other than that Charlie saw her over in a dancing joint in Blanco with someone. He didn't know who it was, said he never got a good look at him but that he was older. From what I can tell, there isn't any solid evidence that he's anyone's husband. Other than the fact that they were over in Blanco."

I shrugged at that. People in Sugar Creek liked to disparage the neighboring towns occasionally, usually due to who was getting more press about their barbecue or who'd won the pie contest at the county fair the year before. It didn't really add up to the fact that she was trying to hide an affair. Maybe she just wanted to go dancing somewhere different?

Cassie took a drink of her tea and gazed out the window a moment before leaning back in. "Find anything out about the business?"

I nodded and swallowed. "I talked to their admin Stacy this morning to place an order for rentals. Boy, she was a character. Said that Trisha and Greg fought about money all the time. She mentioned something about insurance, which was weird. I'm almost positive that Greg told me yesterday that one benefit of storing things on his property was that he didn't have to pay insurance." Shrugging, I took a bite of potato salad. "I guess they could have been talking about a different insurance. I don't really know what types of insurance businesses are supposed to have. Do you?"

She nodded and contemplated. "I don't know exactly about their business. But for the shop, I have liability, which covers people getting hurt at the store. That kind of thing. And then I have property insurance. That's for damage to the store or my inventory. Like if there was a fire or something. Which is probably what Greg was talking about. Seems like something he'd want to pay for even if he stored the rental stuff on his property, but to each his own."

I wondered how I might find out more about the company's insurance. It felt like an uphill battle, though. Who was going to talk to me about something like that? I was a glorified out-of-towner.

"What do you think we should do about the things we found at Trisha's? Should I tell Ty?" Cassie asked, a worried look crossing her face.

I frowned. "I don't know. We should definitely tell the police somehow, right? I mean, it could be important evidence for the case. Maybe it would even get Marlene off the hook, assuming the sheriff knows something more than we do. But I don't know. What if they think *we* killed her and are just trying to mess up the investigation?"

Cassie nodded. "I'm worried about how Ty might react. It wouldn't be too hard for him to figure out that I took the keys from him. I don't want to lose him, Abby! He's so wonderful, and we haven't been together all that long. I know I shouldn't have taken the keys, but it seemed so important. Now I've broken his trust. If he finds out, I'm worried it will all be over."

The look on her face was more than I could bear. "What if we sent the pictures in as an anonymous tip? I could set up a fake email account or something, just say it's from a concerned citizen who knows Trisha and wants to see justice done?"

Her face lightened considerably. "You don't think they'd figure us out?"

"I doubt it. Setting up a fake email is pretty easy these days. And it's not like we're sending them to the FBI. This is Sugar Creek. I doubt they're going to go to the trouble of getting whatever high-powered clearance they would need to track down an anonymous mailer."

I almost believed it. But I knew there was still risk involved. At the same time, there was plenty of risk involved with sitting on what we'd found at Trisha's that morning, including Marlene not getting out of jail in time for the wedding. I didn't want to be responsible for hindering the sheriff's investigation. Not only because I wanted to see justice done for Trisha, but because I didn't want to get arrested myself.

"It's our best option, as far as I can see. We have to do something. I'll send it tonight when I get back to the B&B."

Cassie nodded, and we focused on our food for a bit, chatting about things we hadn't had time to catch up on in the two years I'd been gone. It was so nice to be home with my best friend again. I'd missed her so much when I'd been in L.A. but I hadn't realized how much until I was sitting in front of her.

"What do you know about Sheriff Iverson?" I asked after a while, studying what was left of my potato salad intensely and hoping Cassie didn't notice me blushing.

Cassie didn't answer me, so I looked up and caught her grinning at me. I blushed even harder. "What?"

"You like the sheriff!" She was giddy, and I was sorely tempted to throw my slice of bread at her.

"I'm just curious!"

"And I'm just Marilyn Monroe!" She laughed, and I tried not to scowl. "I'm sorry, Abby. It's just too fun to think about. What if you were with the sheriff and I was with the deputy? It'd be like we were dating the entire police force."

I hadn't put a name to the things I was feeling about the sheriff yet, but once she said it, I realized that I was indeed interested in the possibility of dating him.

I ate the last bite of my brisket, letting the meat melt in my mouth a minute before saying anything. "Do you know if he's seeing anyone?"

She grinned again, clearly thrilled to be right about my interest. "He's single. I don't know much about him, but he hasn't left Sugar

Creek once since he came here from Dallas. He might have a broken heart. Who knows?"

"You've been reading too many romance novels," I said, and she threw her head back and laughed so hard that other diners turned to look at us.

Just then, Janine Yardly came over to our table, a sullen-looking man in tow. "Well, hello there, ladies! I'm surprised to see you out, Abby, what with all the activity over at the B&B."

"Hello, Janine. Yep, just grabbing a little something to eat."

"This is my husband, Frank. Frank, honey, this is Meg's niece Abby. The one I told you about who's here for the wedding? The one who found Trisha's body." Her voice turned down, and I frowned at her for a second before turning to Frank and extending my hand.

"Hi, Frank. Nice to meet you."

He shook my hand, and I noticed his eyes were red and puffy. I wondered what his story was. "Pleasure," he murmured, his gaze flicking to Janine quickly before he looked back at his shoes.

"Any news on the investigation?" Janine asked, leaning in uncomfortably close. I leaned back from her. "I heard they arrested Marlene this afternoon. Must have been quite a scene!"

She sure did have an ear to the ground in this town.

Frank played with his keys as Janine talked, looking more than ready to leave. I couldn't imagine what it must be like to have to live with the amount of gossip Janine dealt out. I wondered how many times he'd already heard this tidbit today.

"Where'd you hear that?" Cassie asked, piss and vinegar in her voice.

"Oh, just around. I have my sources. Anyway, only wanted to say hi. Hope y'all enjoy your evenin'!" Frank tipped his head goodbye to us before following Janine out of the restaurant.

"You think she heard what we were talking about?" Cassie leaned in and whispered after they left the restaurant.

I shrugged. "I don't know. She sure seems to be in everybody's business. I wonder what her deal is."

"Just one of those people, I guess," Cassie said as she stood from the booth and took her plate and cup to a bussing tub in the corner. I followed her and did the same, waving goodbye to Lulu and her staff before following Cassie out to the parking lot. The night was warm, and it felt good after sitting in the cold air conditioning. I was as full as a stuffed pig and satisfied after spending quality time with my best friend. I tried to hold on to the positive feelings, knowing that tomorrow would bring even more drama and chaos.

CHAPTER EIGHTEEN

B ack at the B&B, it only took me a few minutes to set up a fake email account, attach the pictures I'd taken at Trisha's house, write a quick note, and send it to the sheriff's office. It gave me heartburn to do it, and I said a silent prayer as I pushed the send button, but I felt a load off my back as well. Sending the information along was clearly the right thing to do, even if it ended up not being important to the investigation.

I sat at the kitchen table with a cup of peppermint tea as the house settled around me, and tapped my pen on my notebook, wondering what I'd need to do for the wedding tomorrow or if I should even bother. Would Marlene get out of jail in time to have a wedding? I decided to act as if she would so I wouldn't be caught off guard if she was released from jail. We were so close to the wedding that if I didn't keep moving full speed ahead on it, there was no way I'd be able to catch up.

With only two full days left to prepare, I was feeling the pressure. I'd wasted too much time on Trisha's murder and not enough on cooking, and I felt the stress of it building in my gut. I wondered again if I'd thought of everything for the wedding, if I'd planned for enough food for everyone, ordered enough equipment. I'd worked plenty of catering jobs in L.A. but I'd never been responsible for one before. It was a whole new world, thinking about amounts of food to order, the costs, and the timing of it all.

Working an event was a far cry from being in charge of one.

Aunt Meg came in a few minutes later in her bathrobe and grabbed a mug and a bag of tea. "How's it going in here, Abby? Almost ready for bed?"

"Just thinking through the reception a little more. I want to make sure I'm not forgetting anything."

She popped her mug in the microwave and sat down at the little kitchen table across from me. "I hope it happens. I'd hate for you to go through all this trouble and then end up not having the wedding at all."

"I know. It's just so crazy. I can't believe Marlene is in jail right now." I closed my eyes and wiped my hands over my face. It had been an exhausting couple of days and I felt it deep in my bones. "I can't believe all this has happened."

"It's truly a shame. I'm sad for poor Trisha. And I'm sad for Marlene too. I can't imagine she's having an easy time of it right now. And I hate to question the sheriff's capabilities, but I can't believe that she was the one to have killed Trisha. I hope they're looking into other people besides her."

I nodded and thought back to the conversation I had with the sheriff earlier, my heart beating faster as I did. I tried my hardest to ignore the feeling.

Aunt Meg got her cup of tea and came back to the table. She frowned and sighed, fiddled with her cup before speaking. "Things aren't the best around here financially right at the moment. I wasn't going to say anything, but now that this wedding is in question, I hate to say it, honey. But I'm worried." She stared at her hands and I noticed they trembled slightly.

"What do you mean? I thought everything was fine."

"Reservations have been going down now that there are so many short-term rentals on the market. The last year we've only had sixty percent of the bookings we had in 2018. So there isn't as much money coming in. Not only that, but property taxes have gone up like mad. Thanks to the outrageous prices outsiders are paying to buy up all these properties and turn them into rentals, house values have increased, ours included. It's tough for me to keep up with. Uncle Nolan and I bought this house thirty years ago for a fraction of what it's worth now. But the current prices set the tax rate." She sighed. "I thought expanding into events would pull us out of the red enough that I wouldn't have to sell. But if this wedding doesn't go through, well, I just don't know." She sipped her tea and my heart sank. She must have seen it on my face.

"Sorry, honey. I didn't mean to burden you with this. If I have to sell, then so be it. Maybe I'll go buy me one of those little condos in Port A." She laughed, but there was no joy in it.

"Don't worry, Aunt Meg. This is all going to work out." I bit my lip, trying to decide how much I should tell her. I knew she wouldn't be happy about Cassie and my adventures earlier, but I wanted so badly to give her a little hope. "Okay, don't get mad at me..."

She frowned as I said it and I rushed on before I got cold feet. "But Cassie and I went over to Trisha's this morning to see if we could find anything that might help solve the murder."

"Oh, no. Y'all didn't."

I nodded slowly. "We were careful! We wore gloves."

She rolled her eyes, but then leaned in, curiosity getting the best of her. "Did you find anything?"

"We found a whole lot of trash. Goodness, that place was a mess!" I took a sip of my tea and thought hard about our breaking and entering adventures, trying to remember if I'd seen anything that hadn't registered right away.

"We found a man's shirt with a lipstick stain on it. We were thinking it could have been the man who she's seeing right now. I don't know if it's true or not, but we've heard rumors that Trisha was fooling around with somebody's husband." Aunt Meg nodded, and I continued. "We also found a threatening note. It was pretty intense. Here, I took a picture." I pulled out my phone and scrolled to the pictures I'd taken at Trisha's earlier. Aunt Meg studied it for a minute and then I took the phone back and moved to the picture of the financial statement.

"I don't know if this is important or not, but I found it next to the threat. Seemed like something I should get a picture of too, but I'm not sure what it means."

"Let me see," she leaned over and held out her hand, and I gave her the phone. She grabbed reading glasses from the sideboard nearby and slid them on. "This looks like a P&L, a monthly profits and loss statement. Looks like it was from about a month ago," she told me. She frowned as she scanned the lines.

"Why would she have hidden it? Do you think it means anything?"

"I don't know. Looks pretty straightforward to me. Goodness! That is some steep property insurance."

Something clicked, and I took the pages back. "Property insurance?"

"Yeah, that line right there. That's property insurance. But it's way more than I would imagine. They must have a lot more equipment than I'd realized."

I looked at the line again, $550 a month.

"Well, that's definitely odd. Because Greg was just bragging to me yesterday about how he didn't have to pay insurance anymore because he stored everything on his own property."

I pulled up a browser window and typed in the company's name that was listed on the statement. There were many similar names, but nothing was an exact match.

This felt important. Why would Greg say that he didn't pay property insurance when they clearly did? If it was an older statement, it might have been from before he'd built the storage space on his property. But Aunt Meg was right, it was dated February of this year.

She stood with her cup and shook her head. Then she waved her fingers at me. "You girls are somethin' else. Just be careful if you keep snooping. The last thing we need is for y'all to get into trouble." She yawned. "I'm off to sleep. You should be too. You've had a rough day. And who knows what tomorrow might bring us?"

"Good night, Aunt Meg. Don't worry too much, I know this wedding will work out," I said with a conviction I did not feel. I stood and gave her thin body a hug and felt a tug in my heart. "I'll be in soon."

That she was struggling financially was news to me and worry settled even heavier on my shoulders. It hurt me she hadn't confided her troubles before now. Surely there was something I could have done to help more. But I was also deeply sad thinking of the possibility of her having to sell this beautiful house where she'd spent most of her adult life, and where I'd spent most of my childhood. As I stared again at the menu for the wedding that might not happen at all, I resolved to find a way to help her. Even if it meant staying in Sugar Creek for good and giving up my life in L.A.

CHAPTER NINETEEN

I woke up before my alarm the next day. Pale predawn light filtered in through the windows as I slipped into my clothes and headed to the kitchen. I automatically moved to the coffee machine to get it started. Must have coffee. No telling how much of the magical elixir I would need to get through this day, but it was going to be a lot. With only this day and the following left to prep, I knew it would be a bear of a day.

I moved to the kitchen window and for a moment I hesitated, recalling how looking out on the lawn on Tuesday morning had led to Trisha's lifeless body. It gave me a shiver, but I glanced quickly out now, wanting to make sure there were no more surprises waiting for me this morning.

Thankfully, all was still and tranquil, as far as I could tell. No horrific scenes to be found today. I let out a breath, relieved.

After setting breakfast out for the guests, I turned to my wedding tasks and got right to work. As far as I knew, Marlene was still in jail, but I was stubbornly carrying on with my cooking plans, knowing that it would be better to be prepared for a wedding that didn't happen than be unprepared for a wedding that did. I began assembling my ingredients for the artichoke dip that would be part of the appetizer course to be served while the guests waited for the wedding party to take pictures. There would be an open bar and I planned to hire two local people to help me serve the food during the event. If I knew weddings, I knew that this course was often the most important, especially with an open bar. After the appetizer and bar course, there would be a significant amount of the guests who wouldn't even pay attention to the main course or the cake. So I wanted to make sure this course was the one that really wowed.

As I chopped artichoke hearts and grated Parmesan, I thought again of Greg and Trisha fighting over money. Something about what Aunt Meg had said the night before about the financial statement I found at Trisha's house nagged at me. I could have sworn he said he didn't have that kind of insurance, but maybe he was talking about something different. It was strange, though, that their admin Stacy had heard Greg and Trisha fighting over the insurance, too.

What if Greg had been doing something illegal and Trisha knew about it and had confronted him? The note we'd found at her place could have come from him. I hadn't given it much thought before, what with the focus on Marlene and the mystery affair, but maybe Greg deserved more scrutiny over Trisha's death than I'd realized up to now. I wondered if Ryan had looked into him at all. But of course, any sheriff worth his salt would have looked into the business partner right away. I felt silly even questioning it. My mind turned to the anonymous tip I'd sent to the sheriff's office the night before. They must have received it by now. I wondered if it would be enough to get them looking at the business. Or, fingers crossed, give them something that made them realize Marlene was innocent. Thinking about the email made me queasy. I really hoped they didn't have any way to trace that email back to me. I breathed in and out slowly, forcing the fear that dogged me to recede.

The methodical motions of cooking allowed for great contemplation, and the coffee I was guzzling fueled my mind. The idea of Greg killing Trisha over a business spat looked more and more convincing with every stir of my spoon. Bit by bit, the creamy dip came together and so did my theory. I glanced at the clock, wanting to call Cassie and talk it through, but I knew it was still too early for my bestie.

As I spooned the heaping pile of artichoke cheese dip into a container to be baked on Saturday afternoon, Aunt Meg popped in.

"Mmm, something smells delicious in here. At it already, I see," she said, inhaling the garlicky aroma with a smile as she headed for the coffeepot.

"Just doing a little wedding prep," I told her. "Thought I'd get an early start on a few things."

Aunt Meg nodded, pouring herself a generous mug. "Probably a good idea. It's going to be nonstop today." She took a long sip, leaning against the counter. I could tell that the night's sleep had refreshed her. None of the stress I'd seen the night before was present on her face this morning.

A few of the bed-and-breakfast guests began wandering in, drawn by the scent of fresh coffee and hot food. They complimented the appetizing smells as they filled their plates from the breakfast spread I'd laid out earlier.

Maria popped her head into the kitchen a little after eight. "Good morning, Abby! I'm ready to help if you need me. I start cleaning the rooms at nine, but I can help with the cooking until then!"

I smiled at her. "Sure, come on in! I have a mountain of garlic that needs to be peeled!"

Just as she pulled an apron over her shoulders, a commotion in the hall caught our attention. I set the list I was making aside and moved to the kitchen door to peek out and try to see what was happening. Maria came up behind me and we watched as Marlene breezed in through the front door and stopped in the sitting room. A gaggle of women and her husband to be, Derek, trailed after her like a proper entourage.

I grabbed my phone as I made a surprised face at Maria and then dialed Cassie's number. Her beauty sleep would have to wait. This was big news.

After telling her quickly that she needed to come over right away, I shot Maria a look and motioned for her to follow me into the room. We stood in the back near the wall where we wouldn't be noticed. The room was so crowded with Marlene's people and nosy guests who'd also heard the commotion that it was easy for her and me to blend in and not be seen.

Marlene still wore the dirty sick dress they'd taken her away in the day before and she looked downright awful.

"Y'all won't believe the night I had," she began, clearly comfortable being the star of this show. "The police grilled me. Hours of talking. I'm hoarse from it," she exclaimed, making her throat a little more raspy than it had been a moment earlier. I rolled my eyes. Good grief.

Cassie appeared beside Maria suddenly, and I saw that Aunt Meg was hugging the wall with us, too. This was turning out to be quite a show. "Howdy, ladies," Cassie whispered. "What all's going on?"

My eyes widened. "Marlene got released from jail."

"I know. Ty told me. They didn't have enough to keep her."

My eyes widened, and she caught my silent question. She leaned over and grabbed my arm as she said, "they got some evidence last night that helped her case."

Marlene began again, and we shut up to listen.

"It was brutality, pure and simple. They had no reason to drag me away other than that dumb ring they found under Trisha's body," she snorted. "And late last night, I heard them talking about new evidence. They could have let me go then, but decided to make me suffer there all night long!"

She began to cry and just at that moment, Janine waltzed through the front door, a smile on her lips that instantly fell as she realized something big was going on that she wasn't part of. She scanned the room and when her eyes caught sight of Marlene holding court on the couch, she tucked herself into the wall near the door, clearly using our blend-in-with-the-crowd strategy.

"I'm thinking about filing a lawsuit. They really didn't have enough to arrest me at all. And to do it when I was sick as a dog!" She fell back against the couch and bridesmaids swarmed around her. Janine eyed the crowd a moment longer and then slipped back out the front door. Funny, I would have thought she'd want to stick around for the whole show, if for nothing else than to spread it all over town later.

My heart went out to Marlene despite the dramatics, and I booked it into the kitchen where I quickly sliced some cucumber and poured a sparkling water over some ice, then returned to the room. "Here, put these on your eyes. It'll help," I said, holding the cucumbers out.

Marlene smiled up at me and then downed the sparkling water in nearly one gulp. "I need a shower," she exclaimed and popped up from the couch with the cucumber slices in her hand. "Thanks, Abby."

"I'll be back shortly, y'all," she told the rest of the crowd, who seemed to hang on her every word. Clearly, they would not leave until they heard every detail of her arrest. I had a feeling it was going to be a crowded house for the rest of the day. Just what I needed with all the wedding prep that had to get done. I scanned the room one more time and breathed in a deep breath before nodding to Cassie and Maria and heading back to the kitchen to get to work.

It seemed, for the time being at least, that the drama was over.

CHAPTER TWENTY

"Whoa," Cassie breathed out as we got back to the privacy of the kitchen. "That was quite the performance."

I raised my eyebrows and moved around the bar, looking for my trusty notebook. Even though I'd been working on wedding prep still since Marlene got arrested, now that she was released, I felt a huge amount of pressure to get moving on my tasks.

"I wonder if the email got her out of jail," I said. Cassie glanced toward Maria and I smiled. "Maria, this is my friend Cassie. Cassie, Maria is on our team. She's been keeping her eyes out around the B&B. Speaking of which, I was hoping you could keep your eyes out when you're cleaning the rooms today, especially for Donald Watts. Do you know which room is his?"

She nodded and leaned back on the counter, crossing her arms over her chest.

"Don't do anything illegal, though! I don't mean to get you into any trouble. Just have a look around and let me know if you see something that looks out of place." She nodded, and I continued. "I don't know if he has anything to do with Trisha's murder, but he's been acting really suspicious around here and he's the one who originally fingered Marlene. Could have been a coverup or something?" I shrugged my shoulders and pulled a gigantic bag of shelled pecans I'd gotten from Tranquil Valley Farms out of the pantry along with the sugar and cinnamon.

Maria nodded, "I'll see what I can find out." She looked at her watch. "And it looks like it's time for me to begin cleaning. I'll let you know what I find out." She gave us a sly smile and grabbed her cleaning equipment from the pantry.

Cassie smiled too. "Woo, this is exciting! I'm glad the wedding is a go! But I hope it means Ty and Ryan have found someone else to focus the investigation on. I sure would like to see this murder solved." She grabbed a pecan from the bag and popped it in her mouth. "Okay, I've got to get going to open the shop in a second. But what are your thoughts on the murder this morning, Abby? Anything new since last night?"

I told her about the property insurance and my questions about Greg. She frowned when I finished. "Well, that is strange. Hopefully, the email you sent to the station gets them thinking in that direction too. Oh, Ty also said that they got a lock on the tire tracks they pulled from the front of the B&B. He said it was a compact car, probably a sedan. The tire was a Goodyear Assurance brand and looked pretty new. But they wouldn't be able to tell much more than that unless they had the actual tire to compare." She came around and gave me a quick hug. "Okay, got to get going, but keep me in the loop!"

I pondered that as I melted butter and gathered my ingredients to make the candied pecans for the pear and pecan salad. I'd forgotten all about the car that had been parked in front of the B&B the night Trisha was killed. What kind of car did Greg have? I knew he drove a big pickup truck to our place, but that could be a work vehicle. Who could I ask that would know what he drove in his off time? I briefly thought about driving out to his place to have a look around, but that felt too silly. Plus, my day was packed six ways to Sunday as it was. There wouldn't be time for it.

I laid parchment paper on sheet pans and found the biggest mixing bowl in the cupboard, pouring in pecans, melted butter, sugar, and cinnamon, and then adding a dash of nutmeg to the mix. The candied pecans would be a perfect addition to the spinach salad I planned to serve with the main course. And whoever was watching their weight could just push them to the side.

As I ate a couple of the deliciously plump pecans, I couldn't imagine doing such a thing. Food had always been my love, my passion, and after my parents died, my comfort. Saying no to food because of my weight felt like sacrilege. Of course, I'd never tried to fit into a wedding dress, so who knew what might happen in that circumstance.

The pecans went into the heated oven and I glanced at the time, wondering if I should take a shower while there was a lull.

Before I could decide, Aunt Meg came in with a grin as wide as the Brazos on her face. "Looks like the wedding's on! Boy, do we have our work cut out for us." She wiped her hands together and did a little jig and it made me giggle. It was so good to see the worry from the night before gone. "What are your plans for the day, hon?" she asked.

Sipping my lukewarm coffee, I made a face, hightailing it to the machine for a top-up. "I need to go do some shopping. I've been waiting to buy most everything so it'll be fresh, but also because of the tight space. But it's got to happen today. I want to get some more of the food prepped. Tomorrow we'll need to roll silverware, set out all the serving equipment in its place so it's ready for Saturday, and do the bulk of the prep work. I have a big order of food coming from Henderson's tomorrow morning, so I want to double check with Greg about the portable fridge I ordered, make sure they can still get it to us. What about you? What's your day looking like?"

She leaned against the counter and looked out at the half finished setup outside. "I need to get in touch with Greg too and see when he's coming to finish setup. I was hoping to call Louis in for one more mow before the chairs go down. And I need to track down the flowers and lights for the arch. Oh, and I need some more breakfast and happy hour food too for the guests."

"Since I'm already heading to the store, I can pick up whatever you need. Make me a list."

I flipped to a fresh sheet of my notebook, noticing that there weren't too many unused pages left. This wedding had taken its toll on my paper supply. Aunt Meg bent over and began scribbling a shopping list, but before she even got half a dozen items down, Maria rushed in, looking anxious.

"Abby, I think I found something," she said, her voice shaking slightly. She held up a small plastic bag containing a few empty bottles.

Aunt Meg and I exchanged a glance before looking back at Maria. I wiped my hands on a kitchen towel and walked over to her. "What are these?"

"They were in the trash in Mr. Watts' room," Maria said. "I thought they looked suspicious. I didn't touch them. I used some gloves and put them in the bag."

Taking the bag from her, I peered at the empty bottles. They were small and made of dark glass, the kind used for essential oils or homeopathic medicines. There was no label on them, just an odd residue at the bottom that smelled faintly chemical.

I turned the bag around in my hands, my mind racing. "This could be something. I wonder if he poisoned the drinks yesterday, and that's why the girls were sick." I shrugged. "Pure speculation, of course, but it's definitely worth looking into." I bit my lip and frowned. "We should probably tell Ryan."

Aunt Meg frowned too. "Probably. Although I'm not keen on having them sniffing at another guest, not right when we're making progress toward this wedding again. You sure it matters? Maybe it's nothing."

"Wait, there's more," Maria said, reaching into her apron pocket. She brought out a crumpled piece of paper and handed it over. "I found this note under his bed. It looks like some kind of list."

I unfolded the paper, and Aunt Meg peered over my shoulder. We both stared at the list, trying to make sense of the items on it. It read: "sick on tour, laxative in coffee, trip power supply, wine on dress."

There, at the bottom, was a final line: "Food—spill as much as possible, syrup in the salty food, soy sauce in the sweets."

Oh, that did it. Nobody was going to mess with my food. It was time to have a serious conversation with Mr. Donald Watts. "I'll be back," I told Aunt Meg and grabbed my phone. If anything happened when I confronted him, I wanted to be prepared.

Chapter Twenty-One

The wind rustled through the B&B's sprawling backyard as I set out to find Donald Watts. After several minutes of searching, I spotted him near the old, majestic oak tree at the back of the property. He was standing there, partially obscured by the tree's broad trunk, eyeing the tent setup with an inscrutable expression.

"Hey! Mr. Watts! I need to talk to you," I called out, my voice firm and authoritative.

He jumped, startled, and turned around. "Oh, uh, me?" His eyes, wide and a little nervous, looked at me from under a furrowed brow. He was trying to appear innocent, but his reaction made me wonder what he was doing out here. Especially after the list we'd found.

"Yes, you," I replied, squaring my shoulders as I approached him. "I've noticed you sneaking around here. What are you up to?" I demanded, my heart pounding in my chest.

He shuffled his feet nervously against the grass, glancing around as if looking for an escape route. "Nothing, just getting some air," he said, his voice shaky.

I stepped closer, looking him directly in the eyes. My voice dropped to a whisper, hard and unyielding. "I don't think you're being totally honest. Did you have something to do with the wedding party getting sick yesterday?"

His eyes widened in shock. "What? No!" He held up his hands defensively, as if warding off an accusation. "Why would I?"

"Exactly the question I have. Because we found some very incriminating things in your room."

His face darkened. "Why were you in my room?" He took a step toward me and I backed up, suddenly not feeling as sure about confronting him as I'd been when I'd seen the list.

"This is our B&B. We were servicing your room and came upon some things that make you look very guilty. And since there's been a murder on the property, we are keeping our eyes open, like the sheriff asked us to do." Then I acted on a hunch. "Mr. Watts, did you murder Trisha McBride?"

"Of course not! That's ridiculous. I didn't even know her." The accusation had rattled him, just as I'd hoped it would. Now that he was off guard, I leaned in.

"Then why are you trying to frame Marlene for Trisha's death? And why did you make the women on the tour sick?"

His face changed from anger to panic. And then he sighed and looked over my shoulder to the house. I studied him carefully, my gaze unwavering. He seemed scared now, not dangerous. But was it an act?

He let out a long sigh, looking down at his hands. "Alright, I know Marlene, that is true. She and I used to work together. Last month, we were working on a big project as a team. I came up with a truly groundbreaking idea, one that has already saved our company hundreds of thousands of dollars. And you know what Marlene did?" He spat her name out, and I could see just how much anger he held in his heart for the woman. "She took credit for my big idea! And because of it, got the promotion I deserved. You know what I got? Nothing. Zilch. I had to get back at her. I couldn't help it. It wasn't fair!" he whined.

"So you came here to sabotage her wedding? Didn't she recognize you when you showed up?"

"She never paid me much attention at work. Same as now. I was prepared for her to recognize me, and if she had, I would have tried to play it off as a coincidence. But it seems I'm just a walk-on role in the Marlene Lewis show. Not even worth a second glance. So no, she didn't recognize me."

Ouch. That probably stung nearly as much as the work trouble did.

"And so you set out to destroy her wedding. Seems like a pretty difficult way to get revenge for a work scuffle."

"It wasn't just a work scuffle. That project was my life! It was my big chance at moving up in the world, and she stole it right out from under me! Half the time we were supposed to be working together, she was doing wedding stuff, anyway. She wouldn't have gotten any of the credit if she hadn't taken it from under me. I did the work, and she got the reward." I could feel the anger radiate off the man. "But she kept talking about the stupid wedding, and after a while I thought, maybe I'll just take some time off and attend the wedding, even if I wasn't invited. With all her yapping about the dumb thing, it was easy enough to figure out when and where. And it didn't take long for the idea of ruining the event to take hold. I didn't really mean to hurt anybody! And once the murder happened..." he trailed off and looked at the spot where Trisha's truck had been left with her body. "It didn't seem as important anymore. But yeah, I told the sheriff she was fighting with the woman. Why not? It was the truth, wasn't it?"

I scowled at him, even though I was feeling more pity than anger now.

"We found a list, too. Things you planned to do to sabotage the wedding, I'm guessing?" I held the crumpled list out for him to see, regaining steam on my anger as I caught a glimpse of the sabotage he was planning for my food too.

He nodded, shamefaced. "I know. It's silly. Now I see it. But you have to understand. Marlene ruined my professional career! I had to do something!"

I put my hands on my hips and thought. "Listen, this is probably enough to get you arrested. Poisoning people is definitely not legal. But if you agree to leave right now and not come back before the wedding is done with, I won't say anything."

Relief washed over him, and he smiled. "You have to promise to leave immediately, though. And if anything else happens to derail this wedding, I'm going to Sheriff Iverson and telling him everything. So you better be sure that whatever you had planned, you un-plan it. You got me?"

It was unusual for me to be so forceful with anyone. But I needed him to know that I was serious. Especially when it came to my food. If I was going to work my tail off to make this food the best it could be, I was going to be darn certain that nobody sabotaged it.

He nodded and started backing away toward the house. "You got it. I'm sorry, I really am. I didn't really mean to hurt anybody. Thanks for letting me go. I'll get my things right now." There was real fear in his voice and I smiled as I watched him book it to the house.

One problem was solved, but who knew how many more lay on the horizon for me?

———

Heading back into the kitchen, I found Aunt Meg and Maria staring at me.

"What'd you do?" Aunt Meg asked, a look of fear or approval on her face. I wasn't sure which.

I told them about what Donald Watts confessed to me, and that he'd agreed to leave without causing any more trouble.

"Still, I think you should tell the sheriff, just in case," Maria said.

Aunt Meg nodded. "Best to be certain, even if it does cause more trouble."

After a few minutes, the women dispersed, Aunt Meg and Maria moving off to do B&B chores. I sighed as I surveyed the kitchen. It was a mess. But I felt confident now that I had solved the mystery of Donald Watts. It felt like things were beginning to improve. As the morning sun climbed higher in the sky, I threw myself into the whirlwind of tasks that awaited me.

By the time lunch rolled around, a sheen of sweat clung to my skin, and my muscles ached with the fatigue of the day's labor. I managed to sneak in a quick shower, standing under the warm spray and letting it wash away the stress and grime.

I emerged from Aunt Meg's room, feeling refreshed but acutely aware of the ticking clock. The afternoon was slipping away faster than I would have liked, and there was still so much to do.

I had just sat down with a cup of coffee and the ever-growing shopping list when Marlene swept into the room.

"Abby," she began, her voice ringing with a sense of urgency, "I need to ask you a favor."

Uh oh. I didn't like the sound of this. And from her mischievous look, I knew I wasn't going to like what she had to say. I looked up from my task and offered a tight smile. "Sure, Marlene. What can I do for you?"

Her bright blue eyes scanned the kitchen before she leaned in, as though to share a secret. "I need you to add something spectacular to the wedding menu," she said.

I blinked, surprise flooding my mind. "Spectacular?" I echoed, trying to keep my tone neutral, although I felt my pulse skyrocket.

Marlene nodded, her gaze fierce. "Yes, the more extravagant, the better. After all that's happened, I need this wedding to be amazing. It has to be so incredible that everyone forgets about...you know. Everything that's happened."

Her words hung in the air, a palpable reminder of the recent events. I suddenly wished I could tell her about Donald Watts, so that she could appreciate just how much effort I was already putting into making her wedding a success, but I held my tongue. "I see," I said finally. "Do you have something in mind?"

Her lips curled into a thoughtful frown. "Maybe a dessert tower, or a chocolate fountain? Or what about live-cooked gourmet food stations? The kind where the chef prepares the dish right in front of the guest?"

My heart sank as I imagined all the additional work this would entail, but Marlene's pleading eyes held my gaze. "Okay," I said, my voice barely above a whisper. "I'll figure something out. Let me see what I can do. But it's so close now to the wedding that my options are pretty limited." I didn't want her to get her hopes way up, only to be disappointed.

Her face lit up with a radiant smile, but it didn't reach her eyes. "Thank you, Abby! You're a lifesaver!"

As she spun on her heel and left, I couldn't help but feel a pang of sympathy for Donald Watts. Despite her polished demeanor, Marlene was proving to be quite the handful.

I sighed a long, weary sigh, and looked at my shopping list again. I had no idea what 'spectacular' addition I could make to the menu. I was so tired that all the inspiration was gone. Since nothing else was going on, I decided it was time to head to the store. At least I could get the shopping done and look for something to inspire me at the same time.

As I grabbed my purse and headed out the door, I thought about booking myself a massage for the following week. I had a feeling by the time this wedding was complete, I would be a big fat wreck of nerves.

CHAPTER TWENTY-TWO

There were only a few shoppers around as I headed into the grocery store early that evening. I started off taking my time as I worked through the aisles, making sure I was grabbing everything on the list and checking everything out, hoping for some ideas for Marlene's spectacular addition. But by the end of my trip I was nearly flying through the supermarket, trying to get as much of the wedding ingredients as I could before evening set in and I ran out of steam, without so much as a tiny spark of an idea for the new item for Marlene, when I spotted Sheriff Iverson in the freezer section.

My heart pattered as I debated whether to approach him. But he turned my direction before I'd made up my mind and saw me staring at him like a lunatic at the end of the aisle. He flashed me a smile, then headed my direction.

"Abby, hey, good to see you."

I shoved my nervous energy down and tried to present a normal smile rather than the crazed female grin that threatened. "Hey, Sheriff. Ryan. Good to see you too."

"You must be pretty busy now that Marlene is off the hook. Should be quite the wedding. Boy, she can be a handful!" I couldn't help but stare a little as he ran a hand through his brown hair.

"Ha. Yeah. I know all about it. Pressure is on big time for the event. I think she's convinced that if the wedding is amazing enough, everyone will forget about the drama. She talked me into adding another item to the menu, something in her words, 'spectacular'. Which is why I'm here. Lots of work to do."

He nodded. "No doubt. Hey, thanks again for helping us out the last few days. I know y'all are very busy, but it's been nice getting to know you a little."

I glanced in his cart, taking in the frozen dinners, canned chili, white sliced bread and sodas. Not a vegetable in sight. It made me sad to see the food he subsisted on. An idea popped suddenly into my mind. *Oh, boy*. It was a colossal risk, but I knew suddenly that I needed to take it if I had any chance of figuring out what the sheriff's office knew that I didn't. And if I had any chance to get closer to Ryan. Which, I suddenly realized, I very much wanted to do.

"I know this might sound a little forward, but I have some free time tonight. What if I made you dinner? As a thank you for all the hard work you've been doing. I guarantee it'll be better than what you were planning to eat." I glanced again at the frozen meals and the shaker of fake parmesan. Seriously, how was this man living?

"Oh, I wouldn't want to put you out," he protested.

"Ryan, please. Cooking is my job, my hobby, and my passion. It's never putting me out to cook for someone. It's what I love to do most in this world."

He eyed my cart full of vegetables, fancy cheese, and wine. "All this is for the wedding prep. But if you give me half an hour, I can drop this by the B&B and head over to your place."

I blushed then, realizing that I'd just invited myself to this man's house. What had gotten into me? "Or if you'd rather come over to *Primrose House*, I could make something there. Although it's a little crowded at the moment."

He met my gaze and gave me a lovely smile. It was so warm and real that I wanted to melt right into it like the butter in my cart was probably doing as I stood around chit-chatting.

"You can come to my place," he said. "But I'm going to buy the groceries. Just tell me what I need to get."

I smiled as my heart pattered in my throat. There was something about him that made me want to soar right out of my shoes. "Well, what do you like to eat? I can cook almost anything. Depending on what ingredients are available, of course."

He frowned and eyed my cart again. "I'm not picky. But I'm also not particularly creative. Unlike you, from the looks of things."

I smiled, knowing he wanted me to choose. If there was one thing I was certain about after all my time cooking, it was that the hardest part of the job was often figuring out what to cook at all. "What about pork chops?"

He grinned, relaxing. "That would be fantastic."

"I could pair it with a peach glaze and grits. Maybe a blue cheese wedge salad?"

"Wow. I can't believe you just thought of all that off the top of your head. I never would have put those things together, but it sounds delicious."

I grinned at him. "It's one of my superpowers. Now, how about we find some ingredients?"

Five minutes later, he was at the checkout buying the groceries we chose together. I waited for him at the entrance of the store, already checked out, my cart heaped with bags for the B&B.

"Okay, I'll take all this back and meet you at your place," I told him when he finished and pulled his cart up next to mine. He gave me a big smile. "Uh. Where is your place?"

He laughed and gave me the address. I felt his eyes on me as I left the store, and I willed myself not to look back. I didn't know if what I was about to do was brilliant or straight dumb, but I was doing it, anyway. Not only would I have a chance to pick the sheriff's brain on what he may or may not know about Trisha's murder, I could spend a little time with him and see there might really be a spark between us or not. My stomach bounced with nerves as I loaded my shopping into the car and headed back toward Primrose House.

CHAPTER TWENTY-THREE

I'd tried to brush off the suggestive looks Aunt Meg gave me as I'd told her I was going to the sheriff's house to cook him dinner, but in the end I was smiling too big to deny that I was feeling something for the man. She'd wished me luck and promised to hold down the fort. I hadn't brought any nice clothes with me for the trip, thinking that all I'd be doing was cooking and serving food, but I ran around Aunt Meg's bedroom and tried to make myself as presentable as possible with what I had.

The address he gave me was on the other side of downtown from the B&B. It was a pleasant neighborhood of single-family homes with well-kept yards, bicycles, and porch swings. I pulled up to Ryan's house, a charming two-story with a well-kept yard that spoke volumes about its owner. My heart pounded as I took in the sight, the nerves fluttering like butterflies in my stomach. I took a deep breath, gathering my courage before stepping out of my car.

Ryan met me at the door with an inviting smile. "Hey, there. Come on in."

As I stepped inside, the warmth of his home immediately struck me. The walls were painted a soft grey, and he had a few pieces of real artwork hanging on them. The furniture was comfortable and lived-in, a cozy mix of modern and rustic that was both masculine and inviting. A faint scent of pine and something uniquely Ryan filled the air.

"Wow, this place is great," I said, trying to keep my voice casual.

"Thanks. I wasn't sure about buying so soon after moving to town, but the market was good at the time and I had a feeling everything would only get more expensive if I waited. I've always wanted a house like this, so when I saw it, I jumped on it." He scratched the back of his neck, a hint of a blush creeping up his cheeks. "I know the cliche of the cop living in a rundown apartment or whatever. That was never a cliche I wanted to lean into."

His kitchen was a cook's dream, complete with stainless steel appliances and a generous island in the center. I was happy to find it clean and well-organized. There wasn't much more that I appreciated in this world than a clean kitchen.

"From this kitchen, I would say that you like to cook. But from the stuff you were shopping for when I found you at the store, I'm not so sure," I told him, arching an eyebrow as I admired the space.

Ryan chuckled, rubbing his neck. "I try sometimes, but honestly, I'm so busy I don't have the time to spend that I would like. And since it's just me, a lot of times I revert to whatever's easy, even if it isn't the best."

"Well, don't worry. You're in for a treat tonight," I promised, already picturing the gourmet meal I was about to prepare.

He waved his hand at the kitchen. "Please, help yourself to anything. Can I get you a glass of wine? Or can I help with anything?"

I looked through the bags from the store on the counter and pulled out the perfectly ripe peaches I planned to turn into a sauce for the pork chops. "Sure, I'd love a glass of wine. And you can pull out the pork chops and give them a light salt, then leave them on the counter to warm up a tad," I told him as I peeked into cabinets and found a cutting board and a thick cast-iron skillet. Perfect. "We're going to make the sauce for the pork, and then I'll do the grits and cook the chops. While they rest, I'll make the salad."

He poured me a glass of chardonnay and held it out. We clinked glasses and our eyes met as I took a sip. Goodness, he had pretty eyes. So blue it was like looking into the ocean.

"You really didn't have to do this," he said. "I know how busy you are right now."

"Really, it's fine. I could use a break from the B&B, to be honest. Besides, I have to eat and you have to eat, so we might as well do it together."

He leaned against the countertop, watching me with an amused smile.

As I started to cook, the smell of garlic and onions filled the air. I felt a sense of calm wash over me, the familiar rhythms of the kitchen easing my nerves.

"How did you like culinary school?" Ryan asked as he watched me cook.

"It was great, for the most part. Stressful and busy, but I've always loved to cook."

"Really?" Ryan asked, curiosity lighting his eyes.

I paused, looking down at the simmering sauce. The question had hit a nerve, but in a good way. It was a part of my past I hadn't shared with many, but somehow, in this cozy kitchen with Ryan, it felt right.

"I guess it really started when I went to live with Aunt Meg," I began, stirring the sauce gently. "My parents... died in a car accident when I was eight. My brother Devon and I went to live with Aunt Meg and my Uncle Nolan."

Ryan's smile faded. "I'm sorry, Abby. I didn't know."

"It's okay," I assured him, giving him a small smile. "It was a long time ago. But that's when my love for cooking really started. After the accident, everything was so difficult. Sad. Out of my control. But the kitchen... the kitchen was different. It was warm, it was comforting, and after a while I knew what I was doing and that feeling was really nice. Aunt Meg loved to cook. She'd let me help, even when I was just a kid making a mess. Cooking was... soothing. It made me feel better. Like I was creating something good out of all the sadness."

I looked up at Ryan, meeting his gaze. He watched me, not with pity, but with a sort of understanding. It was comforting in a way I hadn't expected.

"Cooking became my refuge," I continued. "And that love just stuck with me, through culinary school and even now."

Ryan was quiet for a moment before he finally spoke. "It seems like you've taken something tragic and turned it into something meaningful."

I nodded, grateful for his understanding. Maybe it was the warmth of the kitchen, the simmering sauce, or the man standing across from me, but for the first time in a long time, I felt like I was exactly where I was supposed to be. I stirred the peach sauce a final time and tasted it quickly, adding a pinch of salt and a little of the white wine from the bottle, ready to change the course of conversation. "Why did you let Marlene go this morning, if you don't mind my asking? Was it because you didn't have enough evidence to hold her?"

Ryan sighed, running a hand through his hair. "Partly," he admitted. "The evidence was circumstantial at best. And honestly, I wasn't all that convinced it was her."

I turned to face him, surprised. "Really? But what about the ring? It was Marlene's ring I saw under Trisha's body, wasn't it?"

Ryan nodded. "Yes, it was. But it was too perfect, too clean. It felt like it was intentionally placed there, not dropped in a struggle or something. How often does someone lose a ring of all things? It was as if someone wanted us to find it and point fingers at Marlene. That fight the two of them had the day before was just too convenient. Partly, I wanted to see if anyone else would stand out with Marlene locked up."

"You were hoping that by arresting her, the real killer might think they were off the hook and slip up?"

"Exactly," Ryan said, his gaze locked on mine. "It was a long shot, but sometimes, that's all you have in situations like this."

"So, have they slipped up yet?"

He threw back his head and laughed. "You should apply for a job with the department, Miss Hirsch. We could use a person with your focus on the team. No, we haven't had any new leads since releasing Marlene. I would have liked to hold her longer, truth to tell, but her mama came in with a storm of high-priced lawyers and that was that."

I pondered what he'd said while I finished making the salad as the pork rested on a cutting board nearby. Then I plated everything up and handed him a plate. "Okay, time to eat," I told him as I followed him to a gorgeous rustic oak dining table where we sat facing each other.

His eyes grew wide as he took a bite of the pork, and I grinned from ear to ear. "Abby, this is incredible. I've never had anything like it."

I knew I was blushing, so I ducked my chin and took a bite of the grits to avoid his gaze. They were deliciously creamy, nice and salty and tangy from the fresh parmesan I grated in at the last minute. "Thanks. I'm glad you like it."

We ate in companionable silence for a few minutes before I got up the nerve to broach the subject of the investigation again. "I know you probably don't want to or can't talk about the case. But is there anything new you've found out about Trisha's death that you could share with me? The reason I ask is...it was really difficult, finding her body. I want so badly for her to have some sort of justice."

He frowned and took a bite of his salad, chewing thoughtfully for a moment. "There isn't a lot I can share with you, unfortunately. It's important that I keep a tight lid on everything. I know you wouldn't do anything to jeopardize our work but I've got to be careful, dot my i's and cross my t's." I blushed even harder at this, knowing that I would, in fact, do things to jeopardize his work. Things like break into Trisha's house. Feeling supremely guilty, I focused my gaze on my dinner.

"We've gotten strange emails. Probably from the killer, but it's hard to know for sure. Anonymous tips. Seems like someone's been in Trisha's house since we were there and found some things. We're looking into it. But that's about all I can tell you at the moment." His brow furrowed, and I nearly choked on my wine, fumbling for how to respond.

Luckily, at that moment, his cell phone rang, and he got up to see who was calling.

"Sorry, I need to take this. Hey, Ty..." He stood from the table and moved down the hall to the bedroom. I sipped the last of my wine, craning my neck to hear what he was saying.

"And did you talk to the accountant?" I heard him say.

Oh, my goodness. He must be talking about Trisha and Greg's business. I nearly fell out of my seat trying to catch the conversation. After impatiently sitting for nearly thirty seconds, I stood and walked a few steps toward the hall where he'd gone. I couldn't help myself. I wondered again if it was my email that led them in that direction or if there was something else about Wildflower Rentals that I didn't know about.

"Okay, we'll head over in the morning. Doesn't sound like there's any reason to do it tonight. That also reminds me, I want to canvass the local tire shops tomorrow, see who might have bought those Goodyear tires. It had to be sometime in the last six months. It's a long shot, but maybe we'll get lucky. Okay, thanks, Ty," he said. I scrambled back to my seat, hoping it wasn't obvious that I was trying to listen.

I composed myself and stuffed a last bite of salad into my mouth before he emerged from down the hall.

"Sorry about that. Hazard of the job. I'm pretty much always on call." I smiled and stood, clearing our plates quickly and taking them to the sink. Rinsing them off, I wondered what to say. I didn't want to let on that I'd overheard his conversation. He came around the counter quickly and took my hand. "Abby, you don't have to clean up too. You cooked such an amazing meal. I'll take care of this later."

Our hands lingered for a moment, his thumb gently circling my palm as we stared at each other. For a second, I thought he might kiss me. But then he dropped my hand and cleared his throat. "I should probably call it a night," he said as he gazed out into the growing darkness. I've got a big day tomorrow. And you do too, no doubt."

I was sad our dinner had ended. The warmth and understanding I'd felt from him was addictive. At that moment, I thought I could be in his company forever. I nodded and tried not to show my disappointment. It was true. I needed to get going. If I didn't get an early start tomorrow, I'd be in serious trouble.

"Thanks for having me over. It was really nice. Maybe after the wedding is over and you solve the murder, we can give it another go."

It sounded more final than I'd meant it to, but it was true. Nothing would happen between us before the drama swirling around us let up. Not to mention, I didn't even live in Sugar Creek anymore. Not for now, anyway.

He walked me to the door, and I heard the buzz of crickets coming in from the warm evening as he opened it for me. We stood together for a moment before he leaned in and gave me a hug. I melted into his arms, loving every second of our bodies touching, but knowing it couldn't last.

He stepped back finally and gave me a smile. "Good luck with the wedding. I know you'll do great."

I nodded and walked out to my car in the low dusk light, wishing more than anything that I could stay longer. But it was not to be.

Chapter Twenty-Four

The day before a wedding is always a hectic day for the caterer. It was my last chance to prepare without the pressure of the event and it was my last chance to double check that everything was in order. Not only would I need to get most of the food prepped and put away properly, I would need to set up all the equipment, the dishes, the silver, and everything else we needed to make this thing happen. My lists had never been so important, and I hugged my notebook to my chest as I made my way to the kitchen through the dark and quiet predawn house.

I stifled a yawn, having gotten very little sleep. All night long, my mind raced with thoughts of dinner with Ryan. But since I was in no position to start something with him, seeing as I didn't even live in Sugar Creek, I tried, mostly unsuccessfully, to push those thoughts away. The murder, however, was a different matter.

As I pulled out the B&B breakfast spread from the fridge, I thought about what Ryan had said about Marlene being a guinea pig of sorts for the actual killer. Assuming the killer had framed her the way Ryan thought, it would make sense that he or she had been at the B&B during the fight between Marlene and Trisha. Or heard about it from someone who was there. My cheeks flushed as I remembered him talking about the anonymous tip. I sure hoped they wouldn't pin that back on me, but at least I was fairly certain that Ryan wouldn't think I was involved in the murder. He would know that I was only trying to help.

I wondered what they would look into this morning. Oh, to be a fly on the wall at the police station! As I arranged the last of the breakfast spread, my mind wandered again to Ryan and how pleasant the night with him had been. It had been a long time since I'd been in an actual relationship. L.A. was too chaotic for me to have any time for one. And I'd only dated one person while I was in Austin for college. That had been years ago. Now my heart pattered as I remembered Ryan's hug as I'd left his place the night before. The crazy thing was that even though I'd only met him a few days before, I could imagine myself with him. He was steady and sweet, something that was harder and harder to find in a man. And I knew without a doubt he was the kind of man who would always be there to take care of me. It was a welcome feeling.

After getting the B&B squared away for the morning, I turned my attention to the wedding plans. I'd decided to just go with a chocolate fountain, assuming I could find one on such short notice, for Marlene's "spectacular" addition. It wasn't particularly creative, but I was running out of time and since she'd suggested it I knew it would make her happy.

I got to work peeling a mountain of potatoes, which was no small task given there would be nearly two hundred people at the wedding. I would par-cook them today and then finish baking them with butter, garlic, and seasoning right before I served them. As I worked, I thought again about Trisha. This morning, I felt convinced that Greg had something to do with her death. I planned to pull him aside and confront him when he showed up later with our equipment. What I wanted to know was whether he was the one who had sent that threatening note. And what was behind the insurance? Was he or wasn't he paying property insurance for his business? I wasn't sure it was the smartest plan, but I needed to see the look on his face when I asked him point blank about it.

"Morning, dear," Aunt Meg said as she shuffled into the kitchen, surprising me. I glanced up to see I'd already been at it for half an hour. "You're up early."

"Lots to do before tomorrow," I replied, scooping what peels I'd already accumulated into a big bucket for the compost. The worms would be happy this weekend.

"Did you have a nice time with the sheriff last night?" Aunt Meg asked, a knowing smile on her lips.

I felt my cheeks grow warm. "I did. The dinner was... nice." I busied myself cutting what potatoes I had peeled and arranging them on baking trays, avoiding eye contact.

"Only nice?" Aunt Meg pressed.

I sighed, turning to face her. "It was more than nice. I really like him, Aunt Meg. But I'm worried about getting involved. I mean, there's so much happening. Not to mention that I don't actually live here. It wouldn't be fair to him or me to start something before I knew for sure that I would be around."

Aunt Meg nodded. "I understand, sweetie. Just follow your heart. If it's meant to be with Ryan, it will happen in good time."

I gave her a small smile, appreciating her optimism. I knew she was right, but my heart and head were conflicted.

"On a lighter note, are you excited about the wedding?" Aunt Meg changed the subject.

"I am," I replied, genuinely looking forward to the event. This was what I lived for. "I'm so glad it's a go, finally. I just hope nothing else happens before we pull it off."

"Don't worry, honey. Things are going to be fine!" Aunt Meg said. I was happy to see her optimism, and I tried to take some in for myself as well. She poured herself a cup of coffee and began helping guests as they came in looking for morning sustenance.

As the B&B woke up for the morning and the house started buzzing with activity, I switched gears and organized what we already had in the fridges to make room for the shipment that I needed to pick up from Georgie. I glanced out the window, wishing Greg would hurry and get here. The portable refrigerator was crucial for the job of rearranging everything, but as the time wore on with no one from the rental company showing, I got more and more nervous.

Maria came in midmorning and asked if she could help. I blew out a frustrated breath, looking at the mess of supplies and equipment all around the kitchen, and glanced at my watch. *10:20.* Where was Greg? "Sure, if you could help me get all of this organized and put away as much as possible, that would be great! I'm waiting for our portable cooler and can't do much more prep work until it arrives because there's simply no room left in the fridge for another scrap of food."

She nodded and smiled, moving to a stack of root vegetables and grabbing a box to put them in. "Have you heard any more about the murder?" she asked as she worked.

I shook my head and leaned in, not wanting the wrong people to overhear. "Not much. Ryan...the sheriff, more or less told me they only arrested Marlene as a decoy to trip up the actual killer."

Her eyes went wide, and I nodded. "Oh, hey, thanks again for finding those things in Donald Watts' room yesterday. Who knows what kind of havoc he might have wreaked on the wedding if you hadn't figured out what he was up to."

"I'm happy to help. I only wish there was more to do. I've been keeping my eyes and ears out, but I have a feeling that whoever killed Ms. McBride wasn't a guest."

I nodded again. I'd had the same feeling for a while and it was growing with every minute that passed without a sign of Greg. What if he'd realized the police were onto him and decided to skip town? Or what if he was the one that Ryan and Ty were talking about looking into and he was being arrested right now? It was a horrible thought, but as cursed as this wedding had been so far, I wouldn't be surprised. I fretted. What would I do if I didn't get those rentals?

After another thirty minutes of worry mixed with wedding prep, I called him. It was nearly eleven, and he was supposed to have been at the B&B an hour ago. But after several tries, his phone only went repeatedly to voicemail. Finally, I called Cassie.

"Hey, Cass. I don't suppose you know where Greg Anderson lives, do you? I've been calling his cell phone, but he isn't picking up. He's late for the equipment delivery and I really have to have that stuff. I'm just going to go over there and get it myself."

"Actually, I do. I delivered a piece of furniture to him a while back. He lives out on FM 459, past the Greer farm. I think the number is 1765, but you'll see it when you get out there. He's got a big barn with a Wildflower Rentals sign hanging on the side. You can see it from the farm road."

"Thanks," I said.

"Hey, before you go," she stopped me right before I was about to hang up. "I was talking to Ty this morning, and he said that they'd figured out who Trisha was having an affair with but that he couldn't tell me who it was other than that it was someone from Sugar Creek and that it was indeed a married man."

Whoa. This was big news. We'd suspected it before, but there wasn't any evidence of it until now.

"I wonder who it is. Did he say if they were investigating him?"

"He said they were looking into some financial stuff and that they thought the affair was a long shot. He wouldn't tell me more than that."

"Alright, call me if you hear anything else! I'm going out to Greg's farm to see if I can get my rentals. And maybe ask him a few questions about property insurance."

"Be careful out there, okay, Abby? For all we know, he killed Trisha. If you start poking around, he might try to kill you, too."

I hadn't thought about it until she said it, but she was right. Greg could be dangerous. But I had to get those rentals, and I was willing to take the risk. He wouldn't be expecting trouble from me, only business. It felt like a safe enough bet to make.

"Okay, don't worry. Nothing is going to happen. I'm just going to find my portable fridge!"

If only I had known how wrong I was.

Chapter Twenty-Five

On my way out the door to find Greg's place, I ran into Marlene.

"Oh! I'm glad I caught you!" I told her. "Do you have a minute to talk?"

She looked half dead and chugged coffee. I had a feeling she and her bridesmaids had been up into the wee hours and wondered if there were any last-minute nerves wreaking havoc. The last thing I needed after all the drama of the week was a bride who didn't really want to get married.

She nodded and headed to a pair of cozy chairs by the front window.

"Are you doing alright?" I asked her, my brows creasing. She really did not look very good.

"Oh, jail! I just can't get the memory out of my mind. I cannot believe that I was in jail! It's not something I thought I would ever say." She looked like she was about to start bawling, and I glanced at the door, wondering if I should flee while I had the chance. But I steeled myself and dove in.

"I'm sorry. I know that must have been a terrible ordeal for you."

She nodded, and I plowed on before she could say anything else. "I wanted to talk to you about the addition to the wedding."

Her eyes lit up, and the tension in my gut eased. Excitement about the menu probably meant that no feet were cold...yet, at least.

"I think your idea of a chocolate fountain is fantastic. I'm thinking one with strawberries and orange slices to dip. We could do it during the passed appetizer period or wheel it out with the cake at the end. What do you think?"

She gave me a big smile and relaxed back into her chair. "I love it. Just spectacular enough to wow the guests."

"Would you like it out during appetizers or at the end?"

She frowned. "What do you think?"

In my mind, I saw all the guests stuffed with chocolate and not interested in eating the gourmet steak dinner I was preparing. "I think as an addition to the wedding cake would be best."

"Whatever you think! You're the expert!"

I was so glad at that moment that she had become agreeable. I didn't know if it was her brush with the prison system or if other things about the wedding distracted her, but I would take it.

"Great! Okay, I'll go get to work. Have a good day, and you might want to ask Maria for some more cucumbers for your eyes. If you get ahead of the swelling, it won't be a problem tomorrow."

She beamed at me as I headed out the door and I felt like I had done some good in the world. Or at least in Primrose House.

It was already warm as I headed out to find Greg. I grew more and more worried as the time passed with no sign of the rental company and now I was vacillating between anger and terror. What had happened?

I followed the directions Cassie had given, pulling onto the farm road slowly, in case there was any police presence. As I did, a tan four-door car raced toward me from the direction of Greg's place. It sped by me and took the curve I'd just turned so fast that I couldn't see who the driver was. The recklessness of it fueled my anger. Why couldn't people drive responsibly, especially on these old country roads? If I'd been twenty seconds slower, that car might have hit me.

I crunched down on my anger as I made my way toward Greg's place. And just like Cassie had said, another minute later I saw the barn with Wildflower Rentals on the side from the road. I turned into the drive and sighed with relief that I didn't see anyone from the police around. So at least he wasn't being arrested. I supposed he could have already been arrested, but I felt I would have heard about it already if he had, given the town's propensity toward gossip.

Greg's truck was in the driveway, the trailer with Wildflower Rentals parked in the spot next to it. I didn't know if he had another vehicle, but the truck was the only one I'd seen him driving. I bet he was home, and he was just hiding from me, the jerk.

Pulling behind Greg's truck, I hopped out of my rental car, determined to get to the bottom of this problem quickly so I could move on to the million other things I had to do today. I bounded the steps of the house, full of piss and vinegar, and rang the bell, looking at my watch again. I didn't have time for this, but if Greg wouldn't answer my call, I had no other choice. If he wasn't able to provide the equipment I'd requested, I would need to make other arrangements from Fredericksburg or even Austin if it came to that. Which would take even more time that I didn't have. Better than using paper and plastic at what was supposed to be a fancy wedding reception, though. Anything but that.

Nobody came to the door, and I pounded loudly and cried "hello?" as I peeked into the open window next to the door. I saw a tidy living room with no signs of life. Where the heck was he?

After a few minutes, I stepped down into the yard and looked around the house, my eyes coming to rest on the barn that sat a little to the left of where I was. I headed in that direction, wondering if Greg was there or at least someone else who might help me get the supplies he'd promised.

I was growing more and more angry with every step. I had enough to deal with between the wedding and the sleuthing and the chaos caused by Trisha's death and having to track down the promised rental equipment threatened to push my fraying temper over the edge.

The warehouse was large, probably two stories, and made of metal siding like a large barn. There wasn't a lock on the big sliding door at the front, so after a second of hesitation, I pushed the heavy metal to the side and walked into the warehouse. It was a massive space with shelves running up and down half of the floor space and piles of tents and chairs and every other bulky rental item imaginable running along the other side of the room. A light was on in the far right corner and I headed in that direction.

"Hello? Greg? Is anyone here? It's Abby Hirsch! I came to see about my rentals!" My voice turned suddenly into a cry as I saw a body hanging from a rope slung over the rafter near the back corner where a makeshift office sat. I ran to the body, which I now recognized as Greg, and pulled the swivel chair near the desk over to help him. But I realized even before I shakily climbed up that Greg was dead. The pallor of his face made that clear.

"Oh dear Lord," I cried, tears popping immediately into my eyes, my whole body beginning to shake. I said it again as I moved off the chair and grabbed my cell phone to call the police.

As I waited for the police to arrive, I looked around, trying my best to avoid the awful body swinging near my head. The desk was neat and mostly bare, other than a piece of paper sitting right in the center. I leaned over and read the typed sheet through my tears.

It had to end. The secrets have been eating me alive and I couldn't go through with another day of my treachery. Trisha was right to question me. I'm sorry for what I did. I shouldn't have killed her. - Greg

And so it seemed we had our answer. But even though it meant that Marlene was definitely off the hook and that the killer was known, it was not an answer that was the least bit satisfying. I glanced again at the body hanging above me and then buried my face in my hands. All of this for money? And not even that much! It was horrible to think about. Life wasted over something so pointless. Not only Trisha's, but Greg's too.

The sound of sirens pulled me out of my stupor and I wiped the tears from my eyes as Ryan and two deputies ran in, along with paramedics. They pulled the chair to the body and quickly cut Greg down, going through the motions of trying to resuscitate him, although it was clearly too late. Ryan watched them for a moment with a frown and then came to me, grabbing my shoulder and easing me into another chair in the corner.

"I'm so sorry, Abby. But I need to ask you a few questions."

I nodded and blew my nose into a tissue he handed me.

"Why were you here?"

"I came to pick up the rental stuff he'd promised to deliver to me. When he didn't show up, I called, but he didn't answer, so I figured I would just come over and see if he was here. We really need to set up for the wedding. He wouldn't answer my calls!"

I felt frantic, confused. Another body, it was too much. I buried my head in my hands and sobbed. Ryan patted my shoulder and then leaned over and pulled me into a hug. It was exactly what I needed at that moment and I leaned in, inhaling the masculine scent of him, comforted by his presence.

"I'm sorry, Abby. I know this is a lot, but I need to ask some more questions. I'll give you a few minutes," he told me as he pulled gently away. He walked off and started talking to his deputies.

I had to pull myself together and find a way past this fresh horror. It wasn't fair! Why did I have to be the one to find Greg's body? One dead body would have been enough for a lifetime, but I'd found two in less than a week! It was an awful thought, and I doubted either of their deaths would leave me for a long, long time.

Not only was I heartbroken and traumatized, I had so many things to do. Things that didn't have anything to do with the bodies I'd discovered. Two families were counting on me to provide for the happiest day of their lives and I couldn't let them down. I needed to pull myself together.

I shook off my feelings the best I could and dried my eyes. There would be time to process all the things that had happened this week after the wedding. For now, there was too much to do.

I watched them wheel Greg's body out on a gurney and then moved over to Ryan's side. "You had some questions?"

He turned to me, compassion all over his face. At least it wasn't suspicion. I saw a few deputies, including Ty, going through the office with gloves and equipment. Why would they be looking for evidence if it was a suicide?

"Yes, if it isn't too difficult for you."

I shook my head. "It's okay, I'd rather get it over with if you wouldn't mind."

He nodded and pulled out a notebook. "Do you remember what time it was when you arrived?"

I frowned. "Maybe around 10:45? I can't remember exactly."

"And when you arrived on the premises, you didn't see anyone else?"

"No, nobody else was here. Although I passed a car on the way over here, seemed like it came from this direction."

Ryan stilled. "Do you remember anything about the car or the driver? The make, model, anything like that?"

"It was a tan four-door car. Maybe a Nissan or Honda, I don't really remember. It was going so fast I didn't get a look at who was driving. The car nearly ran me off the road!"

"Was there anything else you saw when you arrived that feels relevant to Mr. Anderson's death?"

"You mean like the suicide note on the desk? Other than that, I didn't notice much."

"Did you happen to touch the chair that was near the desk?"

I frowned and looked at the desk, where the rolling chair sat in the middle of the floor.

"I did. When I got here, it was pushed under the desk, but I pulled it over to see if I could help him. Sorry I touched it. I didn't realize it was a crime scene..."

"That's okay. I know you were trying to help him. You sure it was pushed under the desk, not over by his body?"

I nodded. "If you don't mind my asking, why are you investigating this? Do you always investigate when someone kills themselves?"

He closed his notebook and glanced behind him at the men at work. "There is some measure of investigation for every death, no matter the cause. But there are a few things here that don't really add up, so I'm making sure to look into everything."

"Like what?"

He put his hands on his hips and sighed without answering me right away. "Unfortunately, because this is an open investigation, I can't answer that. I'm sorry, Abby. I wish I could be more honest with you, but there's a procedure to follow."

I nodded. "I understand. Don't worry about it." Glancing at my watch, my heart skipped a beat. "Do you need me for anything else, or can I go?"

"That's it for now. I'll let you know if we need anything more." He reached out and grabbed my shoulder and gave it a squeeze. "I'm so sorry this happened to you. I know you must be going through a lot right now."

I gave him a small smile. "Me too. It is a lot. But what I really need to focus on is the wedding. I'm going to put this out of my mind as much as possible. Good luck over here. I'll see you later."

He nodded and watched me go, and I tried my best not to let the tears fall again until I made it to my car.

Chapter Twenty-Six

It started to rain softly on the way back to Primrose House and I bit my lip and let the tears fall. The weather fit my mood, but I hoped it would clear up soon. The last thing we needed was a soggy yard for the wedding. Once I pulled back into the parking lot of the B&B, I sat in my car, collecting my thoughts for a few minutes. I wasn't ready to face a house full of people and the inevitable questions that would come. The soft patter of rain against the roof of my car was a comforting rhythm to contrast with the whirlwind of emotions inside me.

Finding Greg's body, so soon after Trisha's, had shaken me more than I cared to admit. It wasn't just the shock of death—it was the sudden, jarring reminder of our mortality, the fragility of life that hung in the air like a ghost. The image of Greg, lifeless and cold, was imprinted in my mind, a haunting echo of Trisha's tragic end. I knew I would never forget either of them.

I grappled with a deep sense of unease. Why them? Why now? I had been piecing together the fragments of Trisha's life, hoping to uncover the truth behind her untimely death. But Greg's suicide, if that's what it really was, complicated matters. Did he kill Trisha over the insurance dispute, as his note claimed, or was there more to this tragic story than met the eye?

I took a deep breath, trying to steady my racing heart. The questions swirling in my mind were threatening to consume me. But I knew I couldn't let fear or confusion cloud my judgment. I had to stay focused, for Trisha, for Greg, for the truth that still lay hidden beneath the surface. And more than that, I had a wedding to cater and barely more than twenty-four hours to pull it off.

I gathered my courage, turned off the engine, and stepped out into the rain, steeling myself for what was to come.

As soon as I entered the lobby, Marlene hopped up from the couch where she'd been sitting with her mother and came toward me. I involuntarily took a step back. What did she want now?

"Abby, there you are!"

"Here I am," I replied.

She smiled, displaying her shockingly white teeth, and I tried not to grimace.

"I know you're already really busy, but I was hoping you might do me a favor."

Here we go.

"I have a million things to do today, as you can imagine. And I was wondering if you might be a doll and stop by the bakery to pick up the cake for tomorrow. Would you believe they aren't open on the weekends?"

I froze, my stomach churning and mind racing. Where on earth were we going to put a wedding cake? I already didn't have enough refrigerator space. But the name of this game was to *please the bride at all costs* and so I nodded.

"Sure, Marlene. I can do that." I managed a smile, though it felt more like a snarl.

"Oh, thank you, Abby! You're an absolute lifesaver," Marlene gushed, her relief palpable. She gave me a quick, unexpected hug, which I awkwardly returned.

As I extracted myself from the embrace, my heart raced. Organizing the wedding was like juggling a dozen balls at once, and picking up the cake felt like someone had just tossed in an unexpected thirteenth. I just hoped the bakery had a nice, sturdy box.

Leaving Marlene, I headed to the kitchen, the heart of all the hustle and bustle. The warm, comforting smell of baking muffins enveloped me as I pushed through the door. Aunt Meg and Maria were sitting at the kitchen table, cutting an enormous pile of plump white roses and placing them in globes of water for table arrangements.

"Abby, honey! You're white as a sheet! What's going on?" Aunt Meg asked. She pulled out a chair next to her, and I collapsed into it.

"Greg Anderson is dead. I found his body."

Maria's hand flew to her mouth, and Aunt Meg reached over and pulled me into a hug.

"Oh no. Oh, honey. That is awful. What happened?"

Before I got a word out, the kitchen door swung open. Janine came traipsing in the back door, collapsing a huge wet umbrella and soaking the floor. I frowned, but she only gave us all a tight smile. "Boy, it's really comin' down out there!"

She sat down at the empty spot at the table, her eyes darting between us with a tension that was almost tangible. I felt a knot tighten in my stomach as she took a deep breath.

"I heard the most dreadful news," she began, her voice shaking slightly. She glanced at me, a flicker of something in her eyes that I couldn't quite place. "Greg Anderson... he's dead."

Aunt Meg's eyes narrowed. Maria continued to carefully cut roses, her gaze fixed on Janine. The room was tense, the only sound the soft patter of rain against the window.

Janine continued, her voice barely above a whisper, "They're saying it was suicide... and that he confessed to Trisha's murder."

Aunt Meg found her voice first. "Janine, where on earth did you hear such a thing?"

"Frank has a police scanner, it's a hobby of his. He heard it over the radio," Janine replied, her gaze dropping to the table for a moment before meeting our gazes once more. So this was why Janine knew so much town gossip so quickly. I wondered if the hobby was really Frank's or if it was all Janine and her addiction to town secrets.

Janine's news hung heavy in the air. Maria looked at me and then at Aunt Meg, trying to gauge our reactions, and then back to Janine, her eyes wide with confusion and shock. "But... but how? Why would he...?" she trailed off, unable to finish her sentence.

"I don't know, hon," Janine shook her head sadly. "I guess he had so much remorse over Trisha that he couldn't stand it any longer."

Aunt Meg was silent, her stern gaze fixed on Janine. She looked like she was trying to read between the lines, her mind working to piece together the puzzle. Her brows furrowed, her lips pressed into a tight line.

Janine shook her head sadly and then stood and pushed her chair in. "I'm sorry to drop this kind of bombshell and then leave y'all, but I have a roast in the oven. I just wanted to come over and tell you the news, in case you hadn't already heard. I know Greg was working on the wedding for tomorrow. I hope it doesn't affect things too much." A look of concern accompanied her words, but there was a smugness underneath the look that didn't sit well with me. I knew that some people lived for gossip, and clearly this was the type of person Janine was. But I couldn't help but wonder what was beneath her desire to talk about everyone behind their backs.

She picked up her umbrella and shook it. "Good luck with the wedding tomorrow. Seems like y'all are really going to need as much luck as you can get." She stepped outside, leaving behind a puddle of rainwater and a room full of worry.

Before I could dive too much into the questions swirling in my mind, Aunt Meg reached a hand over and squeezed my shoulder. "I'm sorry this is happening. Do you want to go lie down for a while?"

I sat up straighter and gave them both a smile that I did not much feel. "It's okay. The show must go on, right?" I glanced at my watch and my eyes widened. "Speaking of which, I have to get a move on. I'm supposed to pick up the supplies from Georgie soon. And now, with what's happened with Greg, I doubt we're going to get the rentals I need. I don't even have space in the fridge to put Georgie's stuff!"

My heart raced as I glanced around the kitchen, wondering what I could do.

Aunt Meg rubbed my shoulder, picking up on my distress. "I can give the Connolys a call and see if they would mind us using their fridges for a few hours," Aunt Meg said. "I know they have some big moveable coolers and things for the parties and tastings that they do. If that doesn't work, I'm sure someone will pitch in. Don't worry about it. By the time you get back, we'll have this figured out."

"That would be an enormous help," I told her as I stood and stretched, trying to get some blood flow back into my legs. Boy, was I tense. "I'll call Stacy on my way and see if there's any way they can deliver what we asked for, but with both Trisha and Greg gone, I doubt it. I'll let you know what she says."

"I just can't believe all of this is happening, especially right now, with this wedding. I don't want to sound selfish, but two deaths do not add to my confidence in pulling this thing off."

"So he killed himself? And he's responsible for Trisha's murder?" Aunt Meg asked as I rolled my neck and readied myself to go back out.

"It looks that way," I began. "But Ryan...Sheriff Iverson...was acting funny when he got there. It was like they were treating it like a murder, not a suicide. When I asked him about it, he said what they were doing was standard procedure. But I have a feeling it's more complex than what it seems."

"That's odd. I wonder what he knows that we don't. From where I'm sitting, it makes plenty of sense that Greg killed Trisha over this insurance thing and then killed himself. What other explanation could there be?" Aunt Meg asked.

"I don't know. It makes me wonder though. What if Greg was actually murdered, rather than killed himself? Why would that happen? Since the note mentioned his role in Trisha's death, it would make sense that whoever killed him would have had something to do with her death, too. Why else bring it up in that note? The note that was typed, rather than handwritten. What kind of person goes through the trouble of printing out a note before killing himself, anyway?"

"I'm sure the sheriff will look at his electronic devices. If he wrote that note, it would likely still be on Greg's computer. Some trace of it, at least," Maria said.

I nodded. "That's a good point. In any case, it's time for me to get going. Hopefully, the sheriff will work things out and find the truth. But I've got a wedding to cook for. See you ladies soon!"

I felt a little better as I headed back out to my car. The rain had cleared, and the sun was out. And talking things over some with Aunt Meg and Maria had really helped to calm my nerves. Which was good, because I had a lot to do.

CHAPTER TWENTY-SEVEN

Before I pulled away from the B&B, I punched in the number to Wildflower Rentals, hoping against hope that Stacy would pick up. I breathed a sigh of relief as I pulled out onto the road and heard Stacy's voice.

"Wildflower Rentals. This is Stacy." Her voice was shaky, and I wondered how much she already knew. I had only found Greg's body less than an hour before, but I knew Janine wasn't the only gossiper in Sugar Creek and it probably wouldn't take long for the news of his death to spread.

"Hi, Stacy. It's Abby Hirsch. I ordered the equipment and stuff the other day for the wedding at Primrose House?"

She started bawling before I even finished. I should have known she would already know about Greg. It didn't really matter how it had gotten to her. I only wished I would have been able to talk to Stacy before she'd found out. Oh well.

"Greg is dead too! Can you believe it? I don't even know if I have a job anymore! Both of my bosses are dead!"

Oh, boy. I wondered if there was any way I'd get the supplies I needed for the wedding. But I also felt supremely guilty for even asking about something so trivial at a time like this.

"I know. I'm so sorry. It must be very difficult for you right now. And I wouldn't even bother you if it wasn't an emergency. But," I took a deep breath. "We're having a wedding here tomorrow afternoon and if I can't get those things I ordered, I'm going to have a huge problem."

She sniffled, and I heard papers shuffling on the other end of the line.

"The police were here earlier. They had a warrant. They looked through everything in the office, took the filing cabinet. I was so scared! And then I found out that Greg was dead!" More shuffling and sniffles came over the car speaker.

"I'm sorry, it's such a mess here. I'm trying to find your paperwork. Oh, here we go. Yeah, I think Nathan should have been on the schedule today to help Greg with the delivery. I could call him and see if he'd be willing to go ahead without Greg. Although I don't know how he'll get paid. I don't know how any of us are going to get paid." Her voice turned down, and I could tell she was crying again.

"Look, I'm happy to pay him in cash whatever I was supposed to pay your company when he shows up. It doesn't really matter to me, as long as the equipment gets here in time for the wedding."

She paused, and I gritted my teeth. "If you could make it happen for me, I'd throw in an extra hundred for you. Cash."

She sighed, and I waited, willing her to say yes. "Let me get in touch with Nathan," she said, her voice infinitely perkier than it had been a minute before. "He was on the schedule for the delivery anyway, so he should be available. I don't know if he has access to the warehouse, though."

"The police are at the warehouse right now, or at least they were when I left. I'll call the sheriff and see if he'll keep it open for Nathan when he arrives. Listen, Stacy. I don't even care about all the equipment right now. What I need as soon as possible is the portable fridge that was supposed to be delivered. Can you pass that message along to Nathan? The rest can come any time today, or even tomorrow. But I really need that cooler."

"Okay, I'll let him know."

"Thanks, Stacy. And hang in there. I know this is tough for you, but things will be okay."

I wasn't at all sure it was true, but I could tell that she needed reassurance. I hung up with her and immediately dialed Ryan's number. It went to voicemail, so I planned to shoot him a text once I got to Georgie's. As I drove through downtown toward Henderson Fine Foods, I caught Cassie's shop out of the corner of my eye and veered suddenly to park there. I didn't have much time, but Cassie needed to know what was going on with Greg. Maybe she could make some sense of things. Or maybe she'd know something more from Ty. I parked and texted Ryan to ask him to please please please let the Wildflower Rental guy have access to the equipment. Then I texted Aunt Meg to tell her that the fridge was on the way. I could only hope it was true as I jumped out of the car and headed toward Cassie's shop.

She met me at the door as soon as I entered. "Ty told me what happened. You have the worst luck, honey!" She pulled me into a hug. "I can't believe you found both of them." She shook her head.

"I know, isn't it awful?"

We moved to the chairs by the window and sat. "I can only stay a couple of minutes. I need to pick things up from Georgie. This day just keeps getting crazier!"

"I could close up early and help you out if you need it. Store has been dead as road kill this week, anyway."

"Thanks for that," I said with a sigh as I leaned back in the plush chair. "I'll probably be fine with Aunt Meg and Maria, but I'll let you know. So what did Ty tell you?"

"That you found Greg's body hanging from the rafter in his warehouse. That it looks like suicide, although they don't think it is."

I leaned forward. "Did he say why they thought that?"

She shook her head. "I asked, but he said he couldn't say, that he'd already told me enough and I better keep it to myself." We both smiled at that. He should know better by now.

"I thought the same thing," I replied. "It looked like he killed himself. But the note was typed. Why would someone type their own suicide note? Seems like an awful lot of trouble to me."

Cassie nodded. "I bet whoever killed Trisha is trying to frame him. Just like they tried to frame Marlene. And they killed Greg to do it."

"It seems too easy, doesn't it? That Greg would admit to killing Trisha the day after they released Marlene from jail and then kill himself. I didn't know him well, but he didn't seem like the type."

"I know. My bet is that the killer is still out there. And now with two murders on their conscience. But who do you think it is? Up to now, our big guess was that Greg killed Trisha. But assuming that isn't true..."

"What about that affair Trisha was having? Could the married man she was seeing have a motive? Maybe he was afraid of being exposed?"

I nodded slowly, considering this. "It's the best explanation if we assume Greg wasn't the killer. If he was afraid of his wife finding out, or if things got complicated... But we don't even know who he is."

Cassie shrugged. "You're right. It's all speculation at this point. But at least it gives us a new angle to consider."

We fell into silence, each of us lost in our thoughts. The mystery was deepening, the list of potential suspects narrowing. I felt more lost than I had before Greg's death.

"I don't know, it's all so confusing," I told her as I rubbed my temples. "As much as I hate to say it, we should probably step away from this and let Ryan and Ty figure it out at this point."

"You're right. But I want to know so badly what really happened! I hope there is an end and an answer. So many murders end up unsolved. I'd hate for that to happen to Trisha."

"What a terrible thought." I shook my head and then stood. "On that note, I've got to run. But let me know if you hear anything new and I'll do the same."

She stood too and hugged me again. "Will do. Good luck with the cooking today. And you better let me know if I can help in any way!"

I gave her a grateful smile and headed back out onto Main Street, willing myself to focus on the task at hand and not on the murder... or murders... that I couldn't make sense of.

CHAPTER TWENTY-EIGHT

A headache was forming as I rushed back to my car and down the street to Georgie's place. I'd been so busy all morning that I'd barely had more to eat than a couple of nibbles of the food I was prepping for the wedding. I was downright starving and walking into Henderson's Fine Foods did nothing to alleviate the problem. The aroma of rich cheeses and olives hit my nose as I pushed into the shop and I felt dizzy.

An older woman was at the counter talking to Georgie. I waved and angled for the side counter, where I spied a tasting spread of sourdough bread and olive oil soaked mozzarella that Georgie had laid out. I tried my best not to scarf it all down, but I was sorely tempted to polish it all off.

As I stuffed my face at Georgie's expense, I listened to the conversation and quickly perked up as I realized they were talking about Greg. How on earth did news spread so fast in this town? Was there a secret pipeline of information I didn't know about? It boggled the mind.

"I was on the phone with him just last night. He wasn't trying to kill himself! Nothing of the sort! In fact, he told me that someone in town was threatening him! He wasn't thinking about killing himself, he was worried for his life. If you ask me, whoever threatened him was the one who killed him," the woman said. There was agony in her voice and I wondered what relation she was to Greg.

"Have you told the police yet?" Georgie asked her as she wiped the counter down. She gave me a quick smile to let me know she saw me, and I grinned and wiped my hands on my pants, but also sheepishly stuffed one more hunk of mozzarella in my mouth. The tender, chewy cheese was absolutely delicious. I grabbed one of the plastic wrapped balls from the fridge nearby, determined to at least pay for some cheese. And have more for later.

The woman shook her head, but her eyes lit up. "I should go to the police, shouldn't I? They need to know. We need to get justice for Greg! Clear his name of this foul suicide accusation."

Before Georgie could respond, the woman turned and headed out the door. She was a woman on a mission.

I frowned as I moved slowly toward Georgie. The idea of Greg being threatened by someone, and it not being Trisha, was important information. It changed everything. If nothing else, it made the idea of suicide much more suspect.

I shook my thoughts off and smiled at Georgie, putting the ball of cheese down. She motioned toward the door where the woman had just left. "That was Greg Anderson's Aunt Lettie. You heard he died, I suppose."

I nodded.

"It really is sad. This community was already reeling from Trisha's death. Now a second one in less than a week? It's making people uncomfortable, even if Greg really did kill himself. Anyway, I guess you're here for your supplies and not for gossip."

"I'll take either. I'm not picky," I told her with a laugh.

"The seafood just came in this morning and it looks incredible. Makes me wish they invited me to the wedding. Then again, with all the drama, maybe not."

She gave me a sad smile and motioned me back behind the counter. I followed her to the back, where she had a walk-in fridge.

"Oh, Georgie! You have no idea what kind of cooler envy I have going on right now," I told her as we walked into the frigid space.

She pulled a couple of boxes from the shelf and put them onto a cart she'd wheeled in.

"This old thing? Every time I come in here, I have this irrational fear that I'll get locked in. It would never happen since I keep it unlocked and there's a panic release button, but my brain doesn't seem to get the message."

"All I've got for refrigeration right now is Aunt Meg's residential fridge. It's probably three decades old. I'm supposed to get a rental fridge delivered but with Greg..." I trailed off and Georgie nodded as she finished loading my cart with boxes of seafood, cheese, and exotic produce.

"Let me know if you don't find a solution. I normally close at three on Fridays and don't open again until Monday, but if you need to store some of this here, I can give you the key."

I gave her a warm smile as I took control of the cart and began wheeling it toward the front door. "Thank you. That's a very generous offer. I'm crossing my fingers for something on the property. I'm already cutting it close on time. But I'll let you know if I need it."

Just before I headed outside with my load, I spied the hunk of mozzarella I'd placed on the counter and grabbed it. "Mind putting this on my tab?" I asked, and Georgie nodded with a laugh.

"Good luck over there! Hope the wedding goes off without a hitch."

"You and me both. Thanks again!"

It was warm and muggy as I finally stepped outside with my overloaded cart. The rain had put a lot of moisture in the air and I immediately started to sweat as I pulled the cart of food to my car and started loading it up. It was tough work on a nearly empty stomach and I made firm plans with myself to sit down and have something real to eat when I got back to the B&B before I did anything else.

My rental car was packed to the brim by the time I got it all in.

There wasn't an inch of space where I could shove in a wedding cake. I would have to drive back to the B&B and put everything away before making a second trip downtown to get the cake. I contemplated sending someone else or calling Marlene and telling her to do it herself, but since I promised to do it, my guilt wouldn't let me shuffle the task off.

The big unknown was the fridge space, though. I hadn't heard anything from Aunt Meg about neighbors or rental equipment arriving yet, and my nerves were on high alert as I headed back with my precious gourmet horde.

CHAPTER TWENTY-NINE

As I navigated my way back to the B&B, my mind spun with the day's events. Finding Greg's body was enough on its own to knock me off kilter. But his aunt's revelation, and the added pressure of the wedding preparations, felt like a whirlwind threatening to sweep me away. Pulling into the driveway, I sighed and took a moment to get my mind focused, the weight of the day pressing heavily on my shoulders.

After a minute to collect myself, I hopped out of the car and grabbed out one box of seafood. I hurried to the kitchen door and nearly gasped with relief as I spied a truck from Wildflower Rentals pulled around back. I threw the kitchen door open and found Aunt Meg talking to a young man who I assumed was Nathan.

"Abby! Perfect timing! Look who's here with a cooler! Where should we put it?"

I hefted the box onto the counter and blew out a breath, looking around the already tight kitchen space. "Can it go outside?"

"Sure, that's no problem, as long as you have an outlet," he told me and then squinted as he looked out the kitchen window toward the yard. "Shade would probably be good too, if you can manage it."

"Okay, give me a minute and we can find a place," I told him and then turned to Aunt Meg and Maria, who both beamed at me. "If you two could pull out the less perishable vegetables and containers of prepped food and get the high end gourmet stuff stored away in the inside fridges, that would be a big help. The stuff from Henderson's is the most fragile, so it needs to get in the cooler quick. The rest can go into the portable cooler once it cools down."

It was a lot of work, but my hopes were high now that we had the equipment we needed.

As I walked out the kitchen door with the person from Wildflower Rentals trailing me, I felt the excited buzz of the wedding. Another two employees from the rental company were there as well, finishing the setup of tables and chairs in the yard. I wasn't sure who had directed them to come back and finish the job, but I was grateful they were here at all.

"This should be fine," I told the man as I turned the corner of the house and found a plug on the house exterior. "What do you think?"

He nodded with a mumbled "sure" and headed back to the house. I ran back to my car and finished unloading the boxes of food, my stomach grumbling more with every trip I made.

Aunt Meg shoved a ham sandwich at me. "You better eat, girl! You're skinny enough as it is!"

I laughed and pulled her into a hug. "You're a lifesaver, Aunt Meg. Once this is over, we're going to celebrate with a big, fancy dinner. Maybe even drive into Austin." I took a quick bite of the delicious sandwich, stacked with homegrown tomatoes, cheese, and country ham, and closed my eyes in satisfaction.

"Okay, I gotta go pick up the cake," I said between bites. "I hate to leave you with this mess." I eyed the countertops full to overflowing with fruits, veggies, and containers. This was beyond a doubt the craziest event I had ever worked.

Aunt Meg made a shooing motion at me. "You don't worry about a thing, honey. We've got this under control."

After giving Maria a few quick instructions on more prep work, I gave them both a big smile of gratitude and headed out to my car with the sandwich. There was no time to sit and enjoy it, but at least my stomach wasn't growling like an angry bear any longer.

Ten minutes later, I pulled open the door of Sugar Creek Bakery, the cheerful bell above the door tinkling merrily as I stepped inside. Immediately, the rich sugary smell of vanilla and buttercream enveloped me and I smiled.

Growing up, the quaint bakery had been one of my favorite places in town. Display cases brimming with rows of cakes, pies, and cookies lined the walls. I vividly remembered pressing my face against the glass as a child, eyeing the lemon tarts and chocolate eclairs Aunt Meg would sometimes buy us for a special treat.

I approached the front counter but found it empty before I realized that the friendly owner, Ellie, was sitting at one of the tables along the wall with Janine's husband, Frank. He was bent over some paperwork with her.

"Oh, hello Abby!" Ellie greeted me warmly. "Marlene told me you'd be in for the wedding cake. Let me just grab it for you from the back."

She bustled away, leaving me alone with Frank. He gave me a polite nod, and I smiled and returned it. I took a moment to study him. He seemed calm, collected, but there was a certain tightness around his eyes, a tension in his shoulders.

"How are the wedding preparations coming along?" he asked, stacking his paperwork together with a deliberate precision. Something about his casual question felt off. It was too ordinary, too mundane for the whirlwind of a day I was having.

"They're going fine, considering the circumstances," I replied, keeping my voice steady. His eyes flickered to mine, a hint of curiosity behind them. I wondered what he knew about the situation with Greg and Trisha. Living with Janine the way he did, he probably knew every detail.

"I heard they arrested Marlene, but then cleared her. That must be difficult to work around, what with the wedding so close," he said, his gaze steady on mine. His words hung in the air, a veiled question left unanswered.

Before I could respond, a flash of gold from his shirt caught my eye.

The buttons. They were distinctive, gold etched with a small star. A memory flashed in my mind—the same buttons on a shirt in Trisha's apartment. My heart pounded as quick realization dawned.

Frank was the man Trisha was having an affair with. Everything tumbled together and made so much sense. His red eyes when we'd met him at the diner. His overly familiar questions about what was happening with the wedding. He had been sleeping with Trisha. But had he killed her?

Just then, Ellie returned with a couple of massive boxes. "The cake is split into tiers. Putting it together is pretty straightforward, but if you need help assembling this tomorrow, you just call me. Hey, I heard that Trisha's partner Greg passed away this morning! What sad news. Do you know what happened?"

Frank's eyes shot up, and a look of absolute terror crossed his face. What was he thinking that created such a reaction? I grew more suspicious of him by the second.

"Oh, I don't know anything." There was no way I was going to share what I knew about Greg. Especially after Frank's reaction. My mind raced with possibilities. Had Frank killed Trisha? Had he killed Greg? I needed to get away, and quickly. I needed time to think, to put it all together.

"What terrible news," Frank finally offered as he rearranged his face, replacing the horror with indifference. "He was a client of mine. A real shock."

I murmured agreement, my thoughts racing even more as I processed the fact that Frank had been the accountant for Wild-flower Rentals. Had he known about the insurance? Had he been the one to let Trisha know about the discrepancies?

The flood of new questions made my face flush.

A sense of urgency washed over me. "Well, I better get going, but thank you, Ellie! I'm sure the cake will be a hit!" I quickly gathered the cake boxes, being careful not to jostle them too much. The last thing I needed was a cake disaster on top of everything else that had gone wrong.

I stepped out of the bakery, my mind buzzing with new information. I glanced at my car, knowing I should take the cake straight back to the B&B. But I needed to process what I'd just learned, and for that, I needed Cassie.

Ignoring my original plan, I headed toward Cassie's shop, just a few doors down from the bakery. My pulse pounded in my ears with each step I took. I couldn't shake the image of the terror on Frank's face when Ellie mentioned Greg's death. It felt like a piece of the puzzle had just clicked into place, and another one had popped up too. I was desperate to talk it through with someone I trusted.

I quickened my pace, the cool breeze doing little to calm my racing thoughts. Running into Frank had been a stroke of unexpected luck. It finally felt like we might be on to something real.

CHAPTER THIRTY

The bell above the door to Cassie's shop chimed as I pushed my way in, barely managing to keep the boxes balanced in my arms. My heart was still racing, my mind a whirlwind of suspicion and revelation.

"Hey lady, what's going on? Whatcha got there?" Cassie asked, her brows knitting together in confusion as she quickly rounded the counter to help me.

"Marlene's wedding cake," I explained, my voice a little breathless. "Listen, something has happened and we have to talk right away. But this cake needs to get into a fridge before I ruin it. Any chance this might fit in yours?"

Cassie's eyebrows shot up, a spark of intrigue flashing in her eyes. "Sure, come on back and let me make some space." She led the way to the homey, cluttered space behind her shop. Filled with charming antique furniture and curiosities, it was a perfect reflection of Cassie's eclectic taste.

As she rearranged items in her fridge, I took a moment to collect my thoughts. My fingers traced the intricate carvings on her old oak table, the cool texture grounding me.

"So, I just saw Frank at the bakery," I began, my voice steady despite the turmoil inside me. "He was wearing a shirt with buttons just like the one we found at Trisha's house!"

Cassie paused, her hand still on the fridge door. She turned to look at me, her eyes wide with surprise. "No way! You think he's the one who was having an affair with Trisha?" Her voice was a whisper, the implication of my words hanging heavy in the air.

"It sure seems that way to me." I began pacing around her shop, my mind buzzing. Each step I took echoed my mounting concern. "Remember the other night at the restaurant? Frank looked pretty upset."

Cassie nodded, following my train of thought. "Right! I noticed that too!" she added, her voice growing more anxious.

"And he's the one who handled Trisha's and Greg's finances. He must have known about the insurance scheme Greg was running," I mused, the pieces of the puzzle fitting together in my mind.

Cassie's eyes widened. "If that's true, then he might have known about the threats Trisha was getting from Greg," she pointed out.

I nodded. "If Greg was the one who was threatening her. We still don't know that for sure."

Cassie let out a low whistle, sinking into a worn-out armchair. "Abby, I think this might be the answer. What should we do?"

I bit my lip. I could feel the acid in my stomach whirling into a frenzy. "We need to tell Ryan and Ty."

Her face fell as she realized the implications. "Oh, boy. If we tell them, they're going to want to know how we know about the shirt. And that means—"

"We'll have to admit to breaking into Trisha's apartment." I finished for her, my stomach twisting.

"And that means that Ty will know I took his keys." The color drained from Cassie's face, and her voice was barely a whisper.

I nodded, sinking into the chair opposite her. "I know. But Cassie, this is too important. Frank... he may have killed Trisha. And Greg too, assuming his death wasn't actually a suicide. We can't keep this to ourselves."

"What about sending another anonymous tip?"

I shook my head. "It would take too much time. I'm worried, Cass. What if Frank killed Greg? What if he's going to kill again? I can't have that on my conscience. We have to tell Ryan and Ty."

"Abby," Cassie whined. "Why do you always have to make so much sense? I better not lose Ty over this. Lord, what was I thinking when I took those keys? Please never let me do something so stupid again."

I reached across the table, gently placing my hand over hers. "We're doing the right thing, Cassie," I assured her, attempting to offer some comfort.

She exhaled, her shoulders slumping as if the weight of the world was upon them, but she nodded. "Okay, okay. Let's do this."

With a sense of shared resolve, we stood up. Cassie went around the shop, turning off the lights and flipping the sign at the entrance to 'Closed'. I helped her with the heavy lock on the door, the metallic click echoing in the quiet street. It felt like we were sealing our decision, making it final.

We moved quickly to my car, where I'd parked it by the curb. Urgency hung in the air between us, making our actions swift and determined. It was that, or chicken out. And we couldn't afford to chicken out, not at this point. As I started the engine, Cassie looked over at me, a mixture of fear and determination in her eyes.

"Boy, they're gonna be mad."

I grimaced as I pulled away from the curb.

———

The drive to the police station was a blur, my mind racing with thoughts and questions. I pulled up in front of the building like a crazy woman, my heart pounding. The old brick building loomed above us and I felt a wave of nausea hit with the realization that I was about to potentially confess to a crime. Things had been so nice with Ryan up to this point. How would he take it when he found out we'd broken into Trisha's house and kept things from him? Not well, I'd wager. Whatever was between us on a personal level might be over before it even began.

Cassie and I jumped out of the car, hurrying along the sidewalk, nearly jogging in our urgency to get inside. I really should have focused on the wedding from the start. This whole thing could have been avoided if I'd just kept my nose out of Trisha's murder from the beginning. But the thought was too little, too late.

Bursting through the station doors, we stopped in our tracks. Ryan and Ty looked up from their desks in surprise. The red-headed dispatcher in the corner stared at us with eyes wide, fingers hovering over her keyboard. Maybe we shouldn't have come in so hot.

"Abby? Cassie? What's going on?" Ryan asked, his eyes narrowing. Whether it was concern or suspicion hovering there, I couldn't be certain.

I exchanged a quick, nervous glance with Cassie. I could see the fear in her eyes, but there was a spark of excitement there, too. The thrill of having potentially solved the puzzle was palpable between us. My pulse was galloping faster than a Kentucky Derby winner.

"We need to talk to you about Trisha's murder," I blurted out, my voice echoing in the quiet room. "We know who the killer is."

Ryan and Ty exchanged a look I couldn't interpret. Whatever they thought about our exclamation, they quickly masked it with professional detachment. Ryan frowned and then stood from his desk and gestured for us to follow him into a back room, which I assumed they used for interrogations. It certainly had the lighting for sweating the truth out of people. Ty followed us in, and Ryan closed the door carefully behind us.

"Alright, let's hear it," Ryan said, his voice steady as we took our seats. He sat down at the desk and leaned back in his chair, his face unreadable. Ty leaned casually against a nearby file cabinet, notebook in hand. The room was thick with tension, our revelation hanging in the air.

I took a deep breath. "When I was at Trisha's house, I found a man's shirt balled up in the corner. It had lipstick stains on the collar and distinct gold buttons and I just saw Frank Yardly wearing a shirt with the same buttons!"

"When you were at Trisha's house? When was this?"

Cassie and I eyed each other, and I squirmed in my seat. Oh boy. Here it was. Time to do or die. "Well, it's a long story, but Cassie and I...we got into her place the day after I found her body."

Ryan closed his eyes and massaged his temple. "Please tell me you are joking right now."

I shook my head sadly. "We were trying to help! I didn't want Marlene to get arrested because of the wedding. And we just thought maybe there was something you might have missed."

Oh boy. That came out all wrong.

"I swear, we were just trying to help." I nudged Cassie, who was shooting Ty a pleading look. He had his gaze back down on his notepad, his face in a deep scowl.

"It isn't Abby's fault," she said and sighed. "Sneaking into her place was my idea."

"I don't care whose idea it was!" Ryan yelled so loud that Cassie and I jumped. "I oughta arrest you both for obstruction of justice! Here I thought you were just innocent bystanders. And now I have to figure out whether I can even trust you. For all I know, one of you killed Trisha!"

"Come on!" Cassie cried at the same time I said, "No!"

"Well, you sure look guilty right about now."

Ryan frowned and crossed his arms. Swiveling in his chair, he looked to Ty, who shrugged.

"Please," I nearly cried. "You have to believe us. We were just trying to help."

"Yeah, we just wanted to help figure out who killed Trisha," Cassie chimed in.

Ryan stood and paced the small space in front of his desk, and despite my fear and excitement and everything else that was coursing through my mind and body at that moment, I also took a heartbeat to appreciate how well his uniform fit his muscular body. I wiped the sweat from my brow.

"So let me get this straight. You two snuck into a dead woman's house, and found what you thought was evidence, and then kept it to yourself for days."

Cassie and I glanced at each other again, and Ryan caught the look. "Oh, Lord. What now?" Ryan said and sat back in his seat.

"I mean, we didn't exactly keep the evidence to ourselves."

"I swear, we were only trying to help!" Cassie pleaded.

"Continue," Ryan said, so clearly annoyed that I flinched. This was not going well.

"I sent you some emails about what we found."

He hit the desk with his palm and Ty audibly growled.

"The anonymous emails? You two sent the emails? Are you kidding me right now?" He rolled his eyes and crossed his arms, turning away to look out the window.

"I'm sorry, Ty," Cassie said gently, turning back to her beau. "Really, really sorry."

"It's not her fault." Now it was my turn to defend my friend. "It's mine. I talked her into it. Don't be mad at Cassie."

Ryan continued to look out the window for an uncomfortably long time. Cassie and I gave each other nervous looks.

"We thought it was the killer sending us those emails. You know how much time we wasted trying to figure out who was sending them? If you'd just told me from the beginning, we might have solved this thing by now."

"We're telling you now," Cassie said, her voice full of resolve. "I know it was wrong, but we wanted to help. It was a bad way to do it. I will definitely admit that. But that being said..." she hesitated and then plowed through. "You all didn't find the clues that we found. And they're significant."

Ty pushed off the cabinet he'd been leaning on and looked at Cassie. "This is so bad, honey. I wish you would have just told me. I thought we trusted each other."

"You can trust me, Ty, you can!" she pleaded. "I just made a mistake. I promise I won't do it again."

"How did you sneak in, anyway?" he asked.

This was going from bad to worse quickly.

"I borrowed Trisha's keys from you," Cassie admitted.

The look of betrayal on Ty's face was almost too much to bear. I squeezed Cassie's hand under the table, regretting that I'd gotten my friend into such an awful mess.

Ryan looked back at us, his face hard. "Let's move on. You said you knew who the killer was."

I took a deep breath. "We believe Frank killed Trisha. He's wearing a shirt with the same buttons as the shirt we found in Trisha's apartment, so we figured he must be the man she was having an affair with, and that means he is the one who killed her..." my voice trailed off as I realized there was absolutely no reason to assume that even if Frank had been having an affair with Trisha, it didn't mean he'd killed her.

Jeez. I really was a terrible detective.

"Okay..." he replied with a frown. "Even if Frank was having an affair with Trisha, which is not a fact but speculation, there is no reason to assume he killed her. Where's the motive? I'm not seeing it."

I shrugged my shoulders. It was a good point. "Maybe he wanted out of the relationship and she was blackmailing him. Or maybe she knew something about him he didn't want to get out." A thought popped into my head just then. "Maybe he's the one who was threatening her!"

Ryan shook his head and glanced quickly at Ty, who shook his head too. "Alright ladies. Thank you for the information. We've got it on record."

Ty nodded at this and pushed off the file cabinet as he closed his notebook with a snap. Ryan stood. "If that's all, we'll let you two go. But please, please. Abby, please, for me, do not go butting into this anymore than you already have. The last thing we need is a couple of amateurs running around, ruining the investigation."

It stung, but I knew it was the truth. I looked at the floor as Cassie and I stood and followed them back out to the main room of the station. The dispatcher in the corner continued to type, but eyed us warily. Cassie made a last attempt at a pleading look toward Ty, but he didn't meet her gaze as he sat back at his desk. Clearly, we weren't wanted or needed at the station, and as we walked out into the afternoon sunshine, I felt about as low as I ever had.

Chapter Thirty-One

We stood together on the sidewalk for a few moments, contemplating our fate. I wasn't sure what to say, and I wasn't sure Cassie wanted to talk about what had just happened. So I changed the subject.

"Do you mind if I pick up that cake a little later? I want to make sure we have enough room in the coolers at the B&B before I take it back. Things are really tight." My pulse climbed as my mind shifted back toward wedding prep and away from our terrible brush with amateur sleuthing.

"Sure, no problem," Cassie replied. She kicked a stone on the curb and it bounced off a light post.

"Look. That was bad. But Ty is going to forgive you. Y'all might even have a stronger relationship now that you've been through this."

She gave me a deeply skeptical look, and I shrugged. "I'm sorry, just trying to make you feel better. Clearly I'm not the person to be taking relationship advice from."

She stopped me before I moved around to my side of the car and gave me a big hug. "It's okay, Abby. You're right, everything will be fine. And I really wouldn't change what we did. I haven't had so much fun in years! Investigating with you has been worth it. Even if we do make terrible sleuths."

I laughed and hugged her back. Despite everything, the thrill of our amateur investigation had brought us closer. It felt like we were kids again, swept up in a grand adventure. I knew I would miss it.

After we said our goodbyes, I began the brief journey back to the B&B. The day had been a constant roller coaster, and my body and mind already felt exhausted. The mountain of work to be done back at Primrose House loomed over me. But as I was pulling away, something caught my eye.

A car parked a little way down the street. It looked just like the one I'd seen pulling out of Greg's place earlier. I slowed to a crawl and chewed on my lip, torn between duty and curiosity. I should really get back to the B&B. But the nagging feeling in my gut wouldn't let me. I swung my rental car around quickly and parked a few shops down from the vehicle.

Stepping out of my car, I surveyed the quiet street, wondering who owned the vehicle in question. I approached the car, my steps light, my senses alert, and I scanned the sidewalk and peered into shops, looking for anyone who might be watching me. The thrill of the investigation was back, and despite everything, I couldn't help but be drawn into its pull.

The closer I got to the car, the more convinced I was that it was indeed the car that had been at Greg's place earlier. It was a light coppery tan color, a four-door Toyota Camry. It was parked in front of the hardware store. I walked by the window and I spied Janine Yardly talking to someone at the counter. Could the car be hers? Or Frank's?

I scanned the car quickly to see if I could see anything on the outside. I had no idea what I was looking for. But the tires reminded me of the conversation that Ty and Ryan had the other night. They were the same brand, Goodyear Assurance. My pulse quickened as I thought about the implications. Not only was this likely the car that was pulling away from Greg's, but it had the same type of tires as the car that had been parked in front of the B&B the night Trisha was killed.

Quite the coincidence.

What I wanted to do was get inside. It was a totally irrational desire, and yet as I hung out on the curb staring at the car, I couldn't seem to talk myself out of it.

I peeked in at Janine through the glass, jabbering away as usual. I glanced back at the car. It was now or never if I wanted to do it. I crossed my fingers and hoped she would keep talking long enough for me to look for any evidence. A note, something of Trisha's, even one of her curly hairs, anything to point to the killer.

Taking one last look at Janine, who still leaned over the counter of the shop, I ducked down, gently pulling the passenger door handle, both thrilled and terrified to find it unlocked. I crouched down and stuck my head in, quickly glancing over the interior of the car.

The car was tidy, almost meticulously so. The leather upholstery was clean, free of crumbs or loose change. There were no coffee cups in the holders, no wrappers or shopping bags on the seats. The dashboard was dust-free, the controls and dials shining under the afternoon sun. The faint scent of lemon air freshener mingled with the more robust aroma of leather.

But something on the floor caught my eye. Something glinted beneath the passenger seat. It was wedged partly under the track of the seat, a small point of light in the car's pristine interior. I reached in, my fingers brushing the cool metal of the object. After a moment of prying, I managed to grab it.

It was an earring. But not just any earring. This was an earring that I'd seen before. I leaned back on my heels and studied the small piece in my hand. *Trisha's* earring.

It was a tiny teardrop, gold with a splash of red at the bottom, just like the one I'd found at Trisha's apartment. This one had a broken clasp. Why was it in Janine's car? It must be Trisha's. My mind raced as I studied the earring. Further proof that Frank was indeed the person Trisha had been sleeping with.

But what did it matter now? I'd told Ryan about Frank, and he hadn't even cared. Maybe he was right. It was just an affair, after all. It didn't mean that he had killed her.

I closed the car door and fell backwards on my butt when I found Janine standing on the other side. Her mouth curled into a sly smile.

"Howdy, Abby."

"Janine! You scared me!"

"Whatcha doin'?" She leaned on the car and watched me scramble to stand up. I gripped the earring for dear life and I could feel her glare through her wide sunglasses.

"Oh, I just... I was just..." Uh oh. What was I doing? It seemed absolutely ridiculous to me in this moment that I had actually snooped in someone else's car right on the street. My sleuthing obsession had clearly gotten the better of my good judgement. I regretted everything and swore to myself I would stop.

"I thought this was Cassie's car," I said lamely. My face flushed with my clearly awful lie.

"Uh huh," she replied. "Believe me, honey. I know a busybody when I see one." She tilted her head back with a big, throaty cackle. And then she turned serious and pushed off the car where she leaned.

"You really should leave the snooping to the professionals. I wouldn't want you to get hurt."

With that, she turned and moved to the driver's side of the car, not giving me another look. She pulled quickly away, leaving me standing on the sidewalk in a cloud of hot exhaust.

Was that a threat? It certainly felt like one. I watched her speed away, still unsure of what the earring meant. I glanced at it again in my hand. It was definitely the same as the earring I'd found in Trisha's bed.

I stood on the sidewalk for a moment longer, the taste of dust in the air and Janine's parting threat making me feel small. I glanced at the earring clutched in my hand, the gold drop a silent testament to a mystery that was far from resolved.

I'd revealed everything I knew to Ryan, and he'd brushed it off. But the earring... this was something concrete, something undeniably linked to Trisha. It was a lead, and it pointed directly to Frank.

Heaving a sigh, I turned toward my car and dusted my bottom as an idea formed. It was a crazy idea. Reckless, even. But I couldn't shake the nagging feeling in my gut, the desperate need to follow this trail to the end. I thought about going back to Ryan and telling him about the earring, but our last visit to the station had gone so poorly it wasn't a real consideration.

Despite my better judgement, I decided I needed to confront Frank about Trisha myself.

I pocketed the earring and walked back to my car, my mind buzzing with plans and what-ifs. As I started the engine, I made a decision. I wasn't done sleuthing. Not yet. Not when I was this close to the truth.

Pulling out my phone, I quickly looked up the address to Frank's accounting firm, hoping he would be at his office. I typed the address into the GPS and buckled my seatbelt, my heart pounding with a mix of fear and determination.

It was a stupid idea, but I was already on quite the roll with stupid ideas for the day. What was one more? I pushed the gas pedal and drove off, the setting sun sinking lower in my rearview mirror every minute, reminding me that a wedding was looming. But my curiosity wouldn't let me be. I had to follow this last lead, no matter how it turned out.

Chapter Thirty-Two

A few minutes later, I was across town near the freeway. I trembled as I got out of my car. Nerves made my hands shake and dread collect in my stomach. I was in a part of Sugar Creek that had once been brush and cactus but now held a sprawling modern strip mall, standing stark against the treeline. The buildings were sleek and uniform, their glass facades reflecting the sinking sun. The parking lot was a sea of gleaming cars, and the distant cloying scent of fast food hung in the air.

I was done playing games. The taste of fear was sharp on my tongue, and I was about ready to puke all over the pristine sidewalk. But I was certain I was doing the right thing. I had to do this for Trisha.

With the image of Trisha's body so cruelly discarded fresh in my mind, I strode towards the building. My hands clenched into fists at my sides, the earring digging into my palm. I reached the entrance, and with a surge of adrenaline, grabbed the door handle.

I swung the door open with more force than I intended. It flew open, hit the wall, and bounced back, narrowly missing me. So much for a subtle entrance.

An elderly woman looked up from the receptionist's desk, her spectacles perched precariously on her nose. She was knitting, the soft click of her needles providing a rhythmic soundtrack to the otherwise quiet office. Her mouth fell open at the sight of me, a half-finished stitch hanging in the air. I must have looked like a whirl-wind, all wild eyes and disheveled hair. I quickly patted down my hair and tried to muster a reassuring smile. The second time today I'd made such an entrance. It was a bad sign.

"Hello," I said, my voice a touch too high, "I'm here to see Frank Yardly?"

She blinked at me, her surprise slowly replaced by professional-ism. Nodding, she put down her knitting and shuffled towards the back of the office. I waited, my heart pounding in my chest.

A few moments later, Frank appeared. His face was a mask of polite confusion, but his eyes were wide with apprehension. He ushered me into his office, a small room filled with stacks of paper-work and family photos.

"I'm not going to beat around the bush, Frank," I spat out as soon as the door closed behind us. The small office felt even more cramped as I began to pace. "I know about you and Trisha."

Frank's face paled, the color draining from his cheeks. His eyes darted to the closed door, a sense of panic flickering in them. The anticipation of what I was about to say must have been terrifying him. I took a deep breath, ready to tell him all I knew.

"What are you talking about?" he asked, sitting heavily behind his desk.

"I know you are the one who's been sleeping with Trisha McBride. That shirt," I pointed at him, "is just like the one we found on the floor of Trisha's apartment with a lipstick smudge. The buttons are too unique. It had to be yours."

He leaned back in his chair and scrubbed a cheek with his palm. He was even whiter than he'd been a moment before.

"Not only that, but I found her earring in your car. Why would it be there otherwise?" I took the earring out of my pocket and tossed it onto his desk.

He picked it up, his beefy fingers handling it delicately. He examined it for a moment before setting it down, his gaze returning to mine with a frown.

"That isn't Trisha's earring. That's Janine's. She loses it all the time. The clasp is broken," he explained, his voice surprisingly calm. "Why wouldn't Janine's earring be in our car?"

The revelation took me by surprise. His explanation caught me off guard, but it didn't mean the affair hadn't happened. I decided to change my tactics and push him more. "Why did you kill her?" I pressed on, my voice barely above a whisper.

"I didn't kill Trisha! She was the love of my life! Why would I kill her?" He broke down with a sob and grabbed a tissue. "I've been heartbroken since she died. We were planning to leave together. Get out of this hateful place, get away from Janine." He spat her name. "Now the love of my life is gone, and I'm stuck here forever. With that woman."

The raw emotion in Frank's words caught me off guard. He seemed genuinely distraught, the image of a heartbroken lover rather than a cold-blooded killer. I studied him, trying to reconcile this version of Frank with the man I'd suspected of murder.

"I... I'm sorry, Frank," I stuttered out, my throat tight. "I didn't mean to upset you." Taking a step back, not knowing how to comfort him, I felt a pang of guilt for my accusations. What a mess I'd made of things.

I excused myself quietly as he continued to sob into his hands. I took a deep breath and stepped out of his office, closing the door softly behind me.

"Y'all have a good day now," the woman in the front said to me as she looked up from her knitting and watched my retreat. I gave her a quick wave, but didn't hesitate. I could not get out of that office fast enough.

I booked it to the car, noticing that the sun was setting beyond the trees. As I started the engine, I made a promise to myself. This was it. No more sleuthing, no more breaking into houses or cars. I was going to focus on what I was here to do: cater a wedding. And maybe, just maybe, I'd get through this weekend without any more surprises.

CHAPTER THIRTY-THREE

When I arrived at Primrose House, the sun was making its final descent, but the place was in high gear. Guests and staff rushed around in every direction. The Wildflower Rentals truck was still parked out back. At least we wouldn't have to worry about the setup anymore. The food was another story, though.

As I came in through the front door, I found the wedding party and what seemed like the entire town, crowded into the front room, noisily taking part in happy hour. A surge of guilt rose in me that I'd left Aunt Meg and Maria alone with so much work. What had I been thinking? I'd gotten so caught up in the excitement of solving the puzzle of Trisha's murder that I'd forgotten my duties.

I blushed hard as I came into the kitchen and found Aunt Meg and Maria slaving away.

"I'm so sorry, y'all," I told them as I threw my bag down and grabbed my notebook from the sideboard. "I got wrapped up in things downtown."

"It's okay, honey. We've got everything under control here. We found your notebook and started doing things that were on the list. I hope that's okay," Aunt Meg replied. She looked dead on her feet and I felt extremely guilty for all my gallivanting around downtown.

I grabbed an apron and opened my page of wedding plans, quickly checking off the prep work that the women had done in my absence. It was remarkable how much they had accomplished.

"I can't thank you both enough. You're lifesavers. How is the portable cooler working? Is it cold enough now?"

"It is perfect," Maria told me as she arranged containers in the fridge. "There is still some space."

"That's good, because I'm going to need to go get the cake from Cassie's place soon."

Ugh. I wished I would have just picked the cake up when I was downtown, but I'd been in a rush to get back and unsure of the cooler, so I'd left it. Now I had yet another errand to run. And more to talk about with Cassie, which was dangerous. Maybe I could send Aunt Meg over to get it. I'd have to see how the next couple of hours went.

I quickly pulled the basket of ripe mangos from the pantry and started peeling them to make the sauce for the crab cakes. As I did, Maria washed up the space where she was working and waved to us. "Time for me to go home," she said. "Daniela will need dinner."

"Of course, honey! I should have let you go hours ago. I'm so sorry," Aunt Meg told her. My cheeks flamed again. How selfish I had been, making Maria stay late to finish the work that I should have been doing.

"I'll see you both tomorrow bright and early! How exciting that we will have a wedding!"

We waved goodbye to her, and then I turned back to making the sauce. My hands quickly grew slippery with juice as I peeled the mangos and diced them into tiny chunks.

As I worked through the fruit, my mind wandered back to the events of the day. The thought of the earring I'd found in Janine's car wouldn't leave me alone. Frank's words echoed in my mind. The earring wasn't Trisha's. It was Janine's. But why had I found the other one at Trisha's place?

I took a deep breath, trying to focus on the task at hand, but my thoughts kept circling back to Trisha, Frank, and Janine. "Aunt Meg," I began, not sure how to approach the subject, "I need to talk to you about something."

Aunt Meg paused her work, giving me her full attention. "What is it, hon?"

I took a moment, choosing my words carefully and then told her everything that had happened downtown. I told her about our talk with Ryan and Ty, about finding the earring in Janine's car, and my confrontation with Frank.

Her brow knit with concern as she processed everything. "Well, I have to say I'm shocked that Trisha was sleeping with Frank! I never would have guessed. He seems so... mild." A smile played on her lips and she grabbed a bottled water and sat at the table, stretching her neck back and forth. "Boy, I bet Janine will be fit to be tied when she finds out. Especially seeing as she's the one who's been walking around town spreading so much gossip about Trisha's murder and Greg..." her voice trailed off.

Our eyes met in surprise and shock as we both came to the same conclusion at the same time.

"You don't think..."

"Janine," I replied quickly as I scooped the pile of diced mango into a container and quickly labeled it with a marker. "It has to be. It makes perfect sense!"

The room fell silent as we processed this revelation. Janine, with her gossip and her bitterness, had every reason to want Trisha out of the picture. The sudden understanding felt like a puzzle piece clicking into place. It was the motive that had been missing with Frank. But the clues could fit Janine just as well as they could her husband.

"Have you seen Janine lately?" I asked Aunt Meg.

She shook her head. "Not since this morning."

I thought back to the look on her face when she'd caught me in her car. She must suspect that I knew something. Was it enough to send her into panic mode? Or would she try to play it cool? I wondered if Ryan and Ty had looked more into Frank, or if they had any idea that Janine might be wrapped up in all this.

"I'm going to call Ryan," I said, biting my lip. I doubted he would take my call, given how we left things at the station earlier. But I had to try. Even though I'd felt certain when Cassie and I had fingered Frank, this was something all together different. Every cell in my body was buzzing with certainty. There was a deep intuition urging me forward.

Aunt Meg paced the kitchen as I dialed once, then twice, and got no answer. I left a voicemail the second time, begging him to call me, and said that it was important. I didn't know what else to do. What if I'd scared Janine enough that she was getting ready to leave town? What if she was going to get away with murdering Trisha?

I couldn't let it happen. Not after I'd spent so much time figuring this thing out. Not after I'd made so many mistakes and caused a rift between Cassie and Ty. If I let this go, and Janine got away, I would never forgive myself.

The thought of facing Janine with this accusation made my stomach churn. But I also knew I couldn't just sit on the theory. I had to do something. What if she was planning to run? Or planning to kill again? The same urgency I'd felt earlier about confronting Frank welled up, and I couldn't ignore it.

I tried Ryan one last time. My call went to voicemail, and I hung up, sending him a quick text. I didn't know if he was mad at me from earlier or simply busy, but he wasn't available and I huffed out a frustrated breath. Looking at the clock and then down at my notepad where a pile of tasks still beckoned, I bit my lip.

"Abby, I can see what you're thinking. You want to go do something about this. But I don't think it's a good idea," Aunt Meg said. "Janine is probably dangerous. If we're right, she killed Trisha, and possibly Greg! It isn't safe."

"I know, Aunt Meg," I admitted, "but I can't just sit around and do nothing. Janine could be planning to leave town, or worse."

"You should at least wait for Ryan to get back to you," Aunt Meg advised, wringing her hands.

"I can't wait," I said, shaking my head, suddenly resolved in my decision. The urgency was like a physical force, pushing me forward. "I need to do this."

Aunt Meg looked like she wanted to argue, but she seemed to see the resolve in my face. "Alright," she finally said, her voice thick with worry, "but promise me you'll be careful."

"I promise, Aunt Meg," I assured her, giving her a quick hug. "I'll be careful. And I'll call Ryan again on the way."

"Call Cassie too. Tell her what's going on and maybe she can try to get ahold of Ty."

I picked up my car keys and saw Aunt Meg's eyes welling up with tears. "Please, honey. Promise you'll be careful," she said, her voice barely above a whisper. "Keep your phone on you."

I nodded, swallowing the lump in my throat. Her concern was palpable, and it echoed my own fears. But underneath the fear was a determination that I couldn't ignore.

As I stepped outside into the cool evening air, a rush of fear and determination swept over me. Fear of the unknown, of the danger I was walking into. But also determination, a burning need to uncover the truth, to make sure Trisha got the justice she deserved.

I paused for a moment and leaned against the car, thinking about Trisha and how her life was cut short. I thought about Frank, heartbroken and lost. And then I thought about Janine, the woman I was now certain was the killer. I pictured her smug smile, the way she reveled in spreading gossip and sowing discord. It fueled my resolve.

It had to be Janine. Why else would her earring have been in Trisha's bed? The fight with Marlene, the threatening notes... it all pointed towards her. She'd been here at the B&B also, the day of the fight. I remembered how we'd caught her with the guest book that first day and now I wondered if she'd been up to something even then.

Starting the car, I took a deep, steadying breath. My hands shook on the steering wheel. I thought about what I was about to do, the danger I was putting myself in. It was terrifying, but I knew I couldn't back down.

I only hoped my realization hadn't come too late, and that Janine was still in town. Letting her get away with murder... the thought was unbearable. I was terrified, but I knew I had to do this. For Trisha, for justice, and for myself.

CHAPTER THIRTY-FOUR

The Stapleton house was about two miles down the road from the B&B and it didn't take me long to get there. It was full night now, and a shiver ran down my spine as I pulled into the drive and my headlights bounced on the old two story brick home. I'd played at this house often as a child. Gabby Stapleton was a year younger than me and we'd spent many days cutting through the brush from her house to mine, playing dolls and house and all the things little girls do.

The house was almost totally dark now, and much more ominous than when I was a child. Whether that was the physical look of the place or simply the realization that a killer likely lurked inside, I wasn't sure.

The car I'd snooped in earlier sat in the drive. Someone, at least, was home. I wondered if Janine was alone, or if Frank was there with her.

I took a deep breath and dialed Ryan's number again, once again getting voicemail. This time, I left him a more detailed message.

"Ryan, I'm at Janine Yardly's house right now. I know you told me to stay out of it, but I am completely convinced that she is the one who killed Trisha. Please come over as soon as you can."

I knew it would make him mad. And I could handle that, as long as he showed up. I didn't let myself contemplate what might happen if he didn't.

I hung up the phone, tucking it securely back into my pocket. I glanced up at the house. It loomed over me, the few visible windows dark and uninviting. A gust of wind rustled through the trees, sounding like hushed whispers in the stillness.

Steeling myself, I climbed out of the car and made my way up the walk to the front door. Each step felt heavy, like I was walking through quicksand. Every creak and rustle made my heart pound in my chest. My hand hovered over the doorbell, hesitating. A part of me hoped Janine wouldn't answer, that I could turn back and leave.

I pressed the bell, the chime echoing hollowly inside the house. Waiting, I held my breath, but there was no answer. I rang again. A knot of fear twisted in my stomach, but I forced myself to stay put.

I was about to turn away when I noticed a faint light spilling from the back of the house. My heart lurching, I moved around the side of the house, my eyes fixed on the faint glow of the light.

The back door was slightly ajar, a sliver of light peeking through the gap. My pulse quickened. I reached out, my hand trembling, and turned the handle. The door swung open easily.

My mind was screaming at me to turn back, to wait for Ryan. But I thought of Trisha, and of the justice she deserved. It filled me with anger to think that Janine might get away, and so I took a deep breath and stepped inside Janine's house, despite the fear.

The interior of the house was dim, the only light coming from a single lamp left on in the living room. The faint glow revealed a scene of hurried packing. Open suitcases lay strewn across the floor, filled with clothes and personal items. Drawers were left open, their contents haphazardly thrown about.

An icy shiver ran down my spine. It looked like Janine was planning to leave town. The thought made my stomach churn. I'd arrived in the nick of time.

Suddenly, a floorboard creaked behind me. My heart pounded in my chest as I turned around to see Janine standing in the doorway, her eyes wide with surprise and suspicion. "What are you doing here, Abby?" she demanded, her voice chilly.

"I...I was just..." I stammered, my gaze darting to the packed suitcases. I needed to keep her talking, to delay her long enough for Ryan to arrive, *if* he was coming at all.

"I came to ask for a favor... about the wedding. I was wondering if we could use your fridge for overflow, since y'all are so close." It was as good a lie as any, and it seemed to work for a moment because her face softened into a smile. But of course I had to go and ruin it.

Gesturing at the mess of suitcases and hurried plans, I tried to sound casual. "It looks like you're headed somewhere, though. Vacation?"

She narrowed her eyes and took a step toward me. I moved back and hit the side of the couch.

"Yes. I've had just about enough of this silly little town and its silly little inhabitants."

I swallowed hard, my mind racing. But suddenly, I decided it was now or never. That there would be no way out of this anyway, so I might as well go all in. "That includes Trisha, I suppose?" I asked, my voice barely a whisper.

She paused, her eyes narrowing at my question. "What are you getting at, Abby?"

"I know she was having an affair with your husband," I said, my voice gaining confidence. "It must have been difficult knowing they were seeing each other behind your back."

For a moment, there was silence. The tension between us was palpable, a ticking time bomb. Then, to my surprise, Janine laughed.

"Yes, I killed her," she said with an eerie calmness. "I waited a long time for just the right opportunity to get rid of that traitorous husband-stealer. It wasn't until she had that fight with Marlene that I could finally do something about her. All eyes were on Marlene and it was only a matter of finding the right timing and leaving behind the right clues. That Iverson thinks he's all high and mighty from the big city, but I knew he wouldn't be able to figure it out if I got it all done just so. And I was right on that count, at least. He went straight for the Marlene bait, never even turned a glance in my direction."

"And Greg? Did you kill him too?"

Janine's eyes were cold, but she laughed. "It wasn't hard to do. A lot easier than I expected, actually. He never heard me coming. Like all the other silly people in this town, he left his doors unlocked, and all I had to do was sneak up on him as he watched tv." She paced and I refrained from pointing out that she'd left her own door unlocked.

"Why?" I wanted to keep her talking, but I truly wanted to understand as well. "Why kill two people?"

"You don't understand! Frank is all I have! I've never worked a day in my life. I have no children. Without Frank, I would have nothing!" She screamed the last sentence, and I tried to take another step back as anger clouded her face. But I only managed to run into the couch once again.

"But you," she said, pointing a trembling finger at me. "You, I never counted on. Who would have expected some goofy woman chef to figure it all out?"

I swallowed, my throat dry as a desert. "The day I met you, you were looking at the room register. You snuck into Marlene's room and stole her ring to plant on Trisha's body, didn't you? You planned it all along."

Janine smiled. "Marlene gave me a fantastic gift when she fought with Trisha. Someone else to place the blame on. It was easy as pie, honey. Her room was unlocked. Surprise, surprise," she stopped pacing and rolled her eyes. "So you might even say it was Marlene's own fault for making it so easy to pin the blame on her. People that stupid should be in jail, anyway. It was almost as if I was doing the public a favor."

"And Greg? You thought you'd just kill someone else when you realized Marlene wouldn't take the fall?"

She sneered. "Greg thought he could threaten me. He knew Frank was sleeping with that slut and he put two and two together about Trisha. So he threatened to turn me into the police unless I gave him ten thousand dollars. Can you believe the nerve of that man? So money hungry, he couldn't tell his right arm from his left. Looks like it cost him in the end, though." She tilted her head back and cackled at her own cleverness. "I got a two-for-one deal. Got rid of his threatening and scheming and found another way to get the focus off of me for Trisha's death. Pretty smart, if I say so myself."

I rolled my eyes and then glanced around the room, wondering if Ryan would ever come. Wondering just how much danger I was in. There was no way Janine was going to let me escape with all of this knowledge. Not after everything she'd already done to cover it up.

She noticed me looking around, and before I could fully process her intentions, Janine reached under the table next to her. In a blink, a glint of silver danced in the dim light. She held a long knife in her hand and smiled the most chilling smile I'd ever seen in my life. My breath hitched in my throat as she lunged at me.

Every bit of my strength mustered, I side-stepped Janine's reckless charge, my heart pounding fiercely in my chest. I couldn't afford to lose focus. Janine spun around and lunged again, her movements frantic, desperate. I dodged again, but this time, her knife grazed my arm. A sharp sting ran up my shoulder, and she took advantage of the surprise to trip me. I landed hard on the couch and she was on me, the knife at my throat.

But before she could cut me, before I had time to react, there was a boom from the side, and I saw Ryan and Ty run into the room, guns drawn, from the corner of my eye.

"Janine, put the knife down this minute," Ryan's voice commanded over my shoulder. I had never been so relieved. He was here. He could help. Maybe I could get out of this alive...

But Janine didn't move. She held the knife to my throat, a wild look in her eye.

"You don't want to do it, Janine. It'll only make things worse. Don't add another death to your conscience. And don't make me shoot you, please."

I watched as he crept slowly in our direction. Janine's gaze drifted between Ryan and me. "You don't know what it's like," she whined, the knife still at my throat but teetering. "Frank is all I have, and he was going to leave me! I couldn't let it happen."

Suddenly, the knife fell to the floor and Janine's hands flew to her face as her tears began to flow.

Ryan swooped in and pulled me away from her with a force that nearly took me airborne. Ty came up behind and hurried to put handcuffs on Janine.

As Ryan led me toward the back door, my legs shook with adrenaline and relief. Janine continued to sob and struggle weakly in Ty's grip as he clicked on the handcuffs. We were all rattled and breathed hard in the tense aftermath.

Ryan's grip on my arms lingered a moment longer than necessary. His eyes searched mine, as if making sure I was truly unharmed. I gave him a shaky nod. It was all I could manage at that moment.

We stepped out into the coolness of the night, and I began shivering uncontrollably.

"You really shouldn't have come here by yourself," Ryan said as we walked slowly toward our cars.

"I know," I replied. Until the moment Janine held that knife to my throat, I didn't really think I was truly in danger. But being that close to death had done something to me. I couldn't believe how stupid I'd been. I was deeply ashamed, and just wanted to climb into my rental car and hightail it back to the airport and the comfort of LA, where nobody knew what a silly person I was.

He reached out to me, his fingers caressing my bare arm, and I stopped, but didn't turn back to him. I couldn't face the disappointment that I knew would be in his eyes.

"I'm sorry I didn't come sooner. I'm sorry I wasn't able to protect you." It wasn't disappointment I heard in his voice, but pain. I turned back to him and he reached for my hand. "I was so worried about you when I got your message."

I looked away as tears gathered in my eyes and then back at him.

"Thanks for coming," I whispered. "I'm glad you got here when you did. That was really scary."

"Of course it was," he said and then pulled me into a hug. It was just about the best thing I'd ever felt, and I leaned in for longer than I should have. Finally, I pulled back and wiped my tears, finding a smile.

"See?" I told him. "I figured it out before you did. I'm not that bad of a sleuth after all."

"Abby Hirsch, you're treading in real shallow water right about now," he whispered, but pulled me back to his chest.

I knew he was right, but I couldn't let it go. "But it's true. You know it is," I whispered into his shoulder.

He laughed, his whole body shaking with it. And then suddenly he bent down and kissed me, making every nerve in my body dance with joy.

Chapter Thirty-Five

Despite the shock I felt after what happened at Janine's, I'd pulled myself together when I'd finally gotten back to the B&B. I don't know if it was the adrenaline that wasn't ready to leave my body after my near death experience, or the fear of Marlene's wrath if I didn't pull the wedding off, but I dug down deep enough to get most of the work finished before collapsing into bed near midnight.

As Saturday dawned, I found a new sense of strength and energy. Knowing that I'd helped catch a killer, and that the wedding was almost over, did a lot to lift my spirits. That, and Cassie jumping on my bed a little after dawn.

"Abby! Wake up, lady!"

"I'm awake, Cassie! But good grief, I can't breathe!"

She sat up and grinned at me, slapping my knee. "I can't believe you didn't call me to go to Janine's with you."

I hid my head under the pillow, not ready for this line of conversation. "Sorry," I mumbled. "I didn't want you to get hurt."

A long pause of silence made me peek out from under my pillow. Cassie had her arms folded across her chest and she frowned at me.

"Oh, but you can go and get yourself hurt? I was worried sick about you! I wouldn't let Ty sleep until he told me every last detail."

I sighed and put the pillow back under my head, then sat up.

"I know, I'm sorry."

She smiled. "Okay, let's not get too distracted here. Boy, have you got some work to do!" She stood up and stretched. "I brought the cake with me. And lucky for you, I'm here to help!"

"Me too," Aunt Meg said from where she leaned in the doorway.

I mentally slapped my forehead, realizing that with all the drama from the night before, I'd forgotten all about the wedding cake. What would I do without my bestie?

Suddenly, I sat straight up, kicking myself for forgetting to set an alarm on such an important day. "What time is it?"

Aunt Meg smiled. "Don't worry, it's only a little after seven. We've got plenty of time."

I was ready for work in a flash, and the three of us convened in the kitchen, which was only in minor chaos. I gave it thirty minutes until full madness broke loose. Luckily, I had a plan.

Skimming the pages of my notebook, I handed out assignments to Aunt Meg, Cassie, and Maria, who had come in a few minutes into my drill sergeant routine, and we all got to work as the B&B kicked into high gear around us. Bridesmaids, gardeners, delivery drivers, and guests ambled every which way, clogging the space. I put my head down, concentrated on the cooking, and tried to tune out the chaos.

The morning passed in a flash, and with all the excellent help I had, I finished the final cooking tasks, including the last minute addition of a chocolate fountain, which I'd borrowed from a caterer in Fredericksburg. As ushers showed guests to their seats, we quietly set the tables in the side yard.

I'd cut it very close. But despite all my setbacks and sleuthing, I'd pulled it off, thanks to a generous amount of help. As the wedding music began to play, we finished setting the tables and the four of us met on the back step, tired but proud of our work.

"I cannot thank y'all enough for the help today. I never could have done it without you," I told the women, holding back tears as I realized just how much they all meant to me, and knowing that in a few days, I would be on my way back to L.A. and away from them all again.

We all hugged, and then scattered, Cassie going home to shower, Aunt Meg moving to the side of the ceremony, Maria to the front of the B&B, and me back to my station in the kitchen. The food was ready to be served, but soon enough, there would be a rush of service to deal with. I'd hired a few local kids to help, and they were already waiting near the tables for the ceremony to end.

After checking on the food, I stepped back outside to watch the end of the ceremony. From the porch I had a perfect view of the couple under the arch and I smiled, relishing the fact that we'd pulled this thing off. It really was beautiful, and despite the complicated feelings I had for Marlene, I dabbed at my eyes as they kissed at the end.

At that moment, Ryan came around the side of the house, decked out in a black button-down shirt and black pants. Perfect server attire. He smiled as he saw me and my heart leapt to my throat as I waited for him.

"I thought you might need some help," he told me as he climbed the stairs, stopping one below me. Our eyes met, and we were finally at the same height. I resisted the urge to reach out to him, but only with great effort. "I know you had a few last-minute hiccups." His mouth twitched, but he had enough grace, or sense, to not laugh out loud. "Which might have been avoided if you'd made better choices about staying out of police business," he added. "But I thought I might see if you could use my help."

I cocked an eyebrow. "I don't know if you're qualified for the job."

He laughed out loud. "I was a head waiter at Duke's in Dallas for three years during college, I'll have you know. I may be a little rusty, but believe me, I'm more than qualified."

"Come on in, then," I said as I turned back toward the kitchen. "I'll show you around."

As the reception got started, the B&B became pure chaos, and I was having the time of my life. I'd sent Ryan out to keep tabs on the hired help, and I grinned at him as I caught his glance midway through the appetizers.

After everything that had happened with Trisha and Greg dying, I couldn't believe he'd sacrificed his Saturday to help me out. He must be dead on his feet after our showdown with Janine. But as he moved around in his crisp black shirt and pants, I couldn't help but admire how good he looked in the crowd. If he wasn't already the sheriff of Sugar Creek, I might try to convince him to come work for me.

"Abby, this food is amazing. You did a great job!" Marlene told me when she found me toward the end of dinner service. She teetered on her very high heels and I worried she might topple over. After the week I'd spent with her, I knew compliments didn't come easy, so I appreciated the kind words. Her life hadn't exactly been a cakewalk this week, either.

"Thanks. I'm glad you liked it."

"I wasn't sure about you. But you proved me wrong. I put a post up on Instagram about the food and the B&B. Good luck." With that, she was back in her element, holding court with her guests.

I spied Aunt Meg beaming with pride on the sidelines and I went to her, leaning over for a hug. It had been a monumental challenge, but thanks to the efforts of so many, our work had paid off.

"Good work, girlie," she told me as she hugged me back. "I think I could get used to this. But only if you'll come back and do the cooking. After watching everything you did this week, I know there's no way I could do it on my own."

I nodded. "If you're serious, I'd love to come back."

"You aren't pulling my leg, are you?" she said, leaning back to look into my eyes.

I shook my head. "It might take a couple of months, but I'm ready to come home. Especially if you're serious about continuing with the events."

She cried in earnest then and I hugged her hard.

It had been a tough week, and the hardest work I'd ever done. But at least now I knew I wanted to come back to Sugar Creek. I couldn't imagine staying in L.A. when Aunt Meg needed me. Being back with my people, and with Cassie, the last week had reminded me of just how much I missed home.

Not only that, but I felt like something was definitely developing with the sheriff, and I wanted to see what might be there.

The only question now was, how soon?

THE END

A charming small town. A peach festival gone awry. A culinary entrepreneur caught in a juicy mystery.

Abby Hirsch has traded in her hectic life in L.A. for a shot at her dream—a catering business in her idyllic hometown of Sugar Creek, Texas.

But when a city councilman dies from poisoning, Abby finds herself in the pits as a potential suspect. Not only is her fledgling business at stake, but the councilman had recently rejected her business license on a technicality, leaving her ripe for suspicion.

Armed with her culinary skills and a knack for gathering clues, Abby joins forces with her best friend, Cassie, and the attractive Sheriff Ryan Iverson. Together they peel back layers of mystery. But can Abby clear her name and serve up justice in time to clear her name and save her business? Or will her dreams of success crumble like a peach cobbler?

Death and Peaches is the second book in the *Sugar Creek Mystery Series*, and is available now!

Order Death and Peaches Now!

Read on for an excerpt from Death and Peaches

Abby's Famous Spinach Artichoke Dip

INGREDIENTS

8 oz package of cream cheese, softened
10 oz package of frozen spinach, thawed and drained
14 oz can of artichoke hearts, drained and chopped
1 teaspoon of Italian seasoning
1 clove garlic, minced
1/4 cup of mayonnaise
1 cup of shredded mozzarella cheese
Salt and pepper to taste

DIRECTIONS

• Preheat your oven to 375°F. Lightly grease a small baking dish with cooking spray or butter.

• In a medium mixing bowl, combine the softened cream cheese, thawed and drained spinach, chopped artichoke hearts, seasoning, garlic, and mayonnaise. Pour the mixture into the prepared baking dish and spread it out evenly with a spatula. Sprinkle the shredded mozzarella cheese evenly over the top.

• Place the dish in the preheated oven and bake for 25-30

minutes, or until the cheese is melted and slightly golden. Allow the dip to cool for a few minutes before serving. Enjoy your dip with crackers, sliced baguette, or vegetable sticks.

STUFFED MUSHROOMS WITH SAUSAGE & BREADCRUMBS

INGREDIENTS
- 1 lb large mushrooms (such as button, baby Bella, or cremini)
- 1/2 lb sage breakfast sausage
- 1/2 cup breadcrumbs
- 1/4 cup grated Parmesan
- 1 small onion, finely chopped
- 2 cloves garlic, minced
- 2 tablespoons fresh parsley
- 2 tablespoons olive oil

DIRECTIONS
- Preheat oven to 375°F
- Gently clean the mushrooms with a damp cloth and remove the stems. Chop the stems finely and set aside.
- In a skillet, cook the sausage over medium heat until browned and crumbly. Drain excess fat and set the sausage aside.
- In the same skillet, add a tablespoon of olive oil and sauté the onion and garlic until translucent. Add the chopped mushroom stems and cook until tender.

- In a bowl, combine the cooked sausage, sautéed vegetables, breadcrumbs, Parmesan cheese, parsley, salt, and pepper. Mix well.
- Arrange the mushroom caps on a baking sheet. Brush them with olive oil. Spoon the sausage mixture into each mushroom cap, pressing gently to stuff.
- Bake in the preheated oven for 20-25 minutes or until the mushrooms are tender and the tops are golden brown.

Heart-Melting Blondies

INGREDIENTS
1 cup butter, melted
1 ¼ cup brown sugar tightly packed
½ cup sugar
2 large eggs
2 teaspoons vanilla extract
2 ¼ cups all-purpose flour
½ teaspoon baking powder
1/2 teaspoon salt
⅔ cup white chocolate, carmel, or regular chocolate chips

DIRECTIONS
• Preheat oven to 350F and line a 13x9 pan with parchment paper

• Combine melted butter and sugar in a large bowl and stir well.

• Add eggs and vanilla extract and stir until completely combined. Set aside.

• In a separate bowl, whisk together the dry ingredients.

• Gradually stir dry ingredients into wet until completely combined.

- Fold in chocolate chips.
- Spread blondie batter into prepared pan and transfer to oven.
- Bake for 25-30 minutes or until a toothpick inserted in the center comes out clean
- Allow to cool before cutting into squares

DEATH AND PEACHES
CHAPTER ONE

T*he stars at night, are big and bright...Deep in the heart of Texas.*
         The song had bounced around my head ever since I'd crossed the border from New Mexico to Texas nearly two days before. As I spotted that first "Don't Mess with Texas" roadsign, the melody intensified in my mind. It was a song that most of us Texans learned in the cradle. Certainly I had.

I'd arrived back in the Texas hill country that afternoon after a very long drive from Los Angeles, my little Honda packed to within an inch of its life with all my worldly possessions. It was the height of summer, nearly July, and instead of the beautiful wildflowers I'd enjoyed when I'd visited in April, the hills were now brown with dead grass and shrub. It was not the ideal time to be moving back to Texas in terms of the weather, but it suited me fine otherwise. Back in April, when I'd visited Sugar Creek to help my Aunt Meg cater a wedding at her B&B, I'd made a plan to move back as soon as my L.A. apartment lease was up. Aunt Meg needed help to get more business, and the plan was to turn her B&B, Primrose House, into an event destination on top of the overnight guest business she currently ran. I was itchy to stop working for other people after culinary school and to start a catering business of my own, so the idea of helping her out with events had turned out to be a perfect fit for the both of us.

Just like when I visited in April, I got a little teary as I pulled off the highway into my hometown of Sugar Creek. The pickup trucks lining Main Street, the statue of a longhorn in the square that kids in town loved to climb, and the sprays of lavender and salvia all around really brought me back to my Texas roots. I'd been gone too long.

But there was nothing that could compare to pulling up in front of my best friend's shop to really pull me into the Texas state of mind. Her antique shop, Divine Finds, was all things Texas, and my heart pitter-pattered with excitement as I parked at the curb outside. I hopped out of the car and stretched a while, so tired of driving that I silently vowed not to sit for the rest of the day. As I walked up the steps, I grinned wide, knowing that I was only seconds away from seeing my best friend Cassie Divine in person once again.

I pushed through the door just as she was coming out of it and we collided and laughed, falling into each other's arms.

"Lady!" Cassie's voice rang out like the sweetest melody, full of warmth and years of shared memories. "Welcome home! Gosh, I missed you!"

I gave her one more squeeze, then followed her inside the shop. The comforting scents of cinnamon and vanilla met me and I instantly felt the weight of the road lift. "I missed you too. It sure is good to be home."

"I bet. I thought you'd be here earlier."

"The traffic through El Paso was no joke. I would have gotten here a lot sooner, but there was a major accident that held everything up."

A few customers meandered through the antique shop, looking at the wares Cassie had collected from countless estate and yard sales over the past year of being in business. She walked back behind the counter and sat on a stool near the cash register, motioning to an overstuffed velvet armchair across from her.

So much for vowing not to sit. But the chair was delightfully soft as I sat and I kicked off my sandals, snuggled into the corner, and tucked my feet under me.

"Well, you're here now! I don't know what you had planned for the night, but I was thinking we could go over to Lulu's for dinner after a while."

I nodded. "That sounds great. First, I want to unpack a little and I was thinking about heading over to Primrose House to visit Aunt Meg for a bit. Maybe we could do that on the way to dinner, if you don't mind?"

"Of course!"

We caught up, Cassie telling me about adventures in antiquing and I telling her the details of the very long drive I'd just finished. We were deep in conversation when two women approached to pay for their purchases. They were in the middle of a lively discussion, their voices tinged with disbelief, as Cassie stood to ring them up.

"I still can't believe it," the first woman said, shaking her head as she placed a vintage teapot on the counter. "A fistfight, right there in the council chambers!"

Her companion, clutching a set of embroidered napkins, chimed in. "I know, right? I thought those council meetings were about as dull as a mashed-potato sandwich, but today was like something out of a TV drama. Councilman Landers and Councilman Weiss, going at it! They're way too old to act that way, if you ask me. They should be ashamed of themselves, grown men acting like teenagers."

Cassie wrapped the teapot carefully in paper and chimed in. "A fistfight? That's crazy! What over?"

The first woman shrugged as she handed over her credit card. "Something about that bill they're trying to pass. It's caused quite the stir. I wish everybody would just simmer down. The heat is going to their heads."

"Yeah, more than likely," her friend added, "although I've heard that bill might change the whole landscape of Sugar Creek, especially for small businesses. So it makes sense they're riled, I suppose."

"I know the bill you're talking about. Seems like everyone in town is up in arms. You're right, if it passes, it'll be mighty hard to keep the big franchises from moving in and changing things," Cassie said.

The women nodded as they pulled out their wallets to pay.

One of them leaned into Cassie. "I heard Councilman Weiss is being bribed by one of those big lobbyists from Austin." She glanced around the shop quickly. "Don't say you heard it from me, though."

Cassie handed the women their purchases, her brow furrowed. "I hope it's just a rumor. He sure has a lot of power around here. But I guess that would make sense why there's so much fighting. Time'll tell, right?"

The women nodded and smiled.

"Thanks for coming in, ladies. Take care now," Cassie told them with a wave and a smile before sitting back down with me.

As the women left, I turned to Cassie, my curiosity piqued. "What was that about? A bill changing the landscape for small businesses?"

Cassie sighed, leaning back against the counter. "Yeah, there's been talk around town. This new bill, if passed, could open the doors for big franchises to come in. It's a real threat to mom and pop places in town. That's why things are getting heated. Some council members are all for it, thinking it'll bring growth. Most, though, are worried it'll hurt the charm and character of Sugar Creek."

I felt a twinge of concern, thinking about my own plans to start a small catering business. "Sounds serious. I should probably look into it before I go apply for my business license."

Cassie gave a small, reassuring smile. "Don't worry *too* much. This town's always been about supporting its own. Even if the bill gets passed, I don't think it'll be as bad as some folks are making it out to be. But it sure has people's tails up."

Before I could say another thing, the chime sounded from the front of the shop. "Yoo hoo!" A call floated back to us and Cassie jumped up. I would know that voice anywhere, and I jumped up too.

Aunt Meg and her employee Maria, who I'd become close with in April, made their way back behind the counter, all smiles.

I grinned, my heart melting, when I saw the woman who'd practically raised me. I squealed and gave them both big hugs. "You didn't have to come over. I was planning on visiting the B&B in a bit."

Aunt Meg waved a hand. "It's no problem, honey. I know you've been in that car for days. And I just couldn't wait." She squealed and squeezed my hand, and I smiled. "Our girl is back for good!"

Cassie pulled two more chairs over and we all sat and caught up for a few minutes. Aunt Meg told a story about a toilet leak that had us all laughing, and Maria told us about her daughter preparing for a trip to Dallas with a school group.

After a while, I leaned in to Aunt Meg. "I have a few ideas for the B&B I want to run by you. I had a lot of time to think on the drive," I said with a laugh.

"I can't wait to hear them! We need all the help we can get. But you must be dead-dog tired. Why don't you stop by in the morning and we can let our imaginations run wild."

I nodded. It was true. The drive had taken a lot out of me. But I was buzzing with creative energy and excitement to get my business off the ground. "Okay. It'll have to be early though. I have a lot on my plate since the Peach Festival is the day after tomorrow."

Maria lit up at that. "Oh, I've heard so much about the festival. I plan to take Daniela. Will you be cooking for it?"

"Yep. I signed up as soon as I knew I'd be coming back for sure. The Peachy Keen contest is what I'm angling for. It's the biggest cooking competition in Sugar Creek. Best peach related entry wins. The Peachy Keen title goes pretty far in this town, so I thought it would be a good brag for my new catering business. And I can hand out samples and business cards to people at the festival. Hopefully, I can get some business flowing right away."

I turned back to Aunt Meg. "Tomorrow I have to do most of the cooking for the festival, but I also need to stop by town hall and file my paperwork for a business license. It's all filled out. I just need to go turn it in. I also need to stop by Wild Hare in the morning. Mark and Sheila said I could use their van for the festival, so I can drop by the B&B before I go pick it up."

Mark and Sheila Connoly had been our neighbors since I was a child. They owned Wild Hare Winery, a beautiful artisan winery near Primrose House that had grown considerably with the influx of tourists over the last decade or so.

"That'll be fine. I should be around until noon at least. I've got a Zumba class at one though, so make sure to come before then." It wasn't a surprise. Aunt Meg was in her late sixties, but she had more spunk and energy than most teenagers I knew.

After a few more minutes, Aunt Meg stood, and Maria followed suit. "We won't keep you girls. We just wanted to drop by and say hi, and we've got to get back to the B&B to set up for happy hour. Hope y'all have a good night. And don't stay up all night long gabbing like you did when you were girls. Y'all need your rest!"

Cassie and I laughed, knowing that in all likelihood we would do exactly that—stay up all night gabbing.

"I'll come by in the morning and we can talk business," I told Aunt Meg, and she grabbed me for another hug, nearly squeezing the daylights out of me.

"Get some rest. I'll see you in the morning!"

Cassie followed them to the door, flipping the closed sign and locking it behind them. "Okay! I know it's a little early, but I declare that business hours are over. Time to have ourselves some fun!"

Order Death and Peaches now!

Every Review Counts!

Thank you for taking the time to read this book! I truly hope you enjoyed it!

If you wouldn't mind too much, I would be incredibly grateful if you could take a few minutes to leave an honest review on Goodreads or the retailer you purchased this book from. Your feedback will help other readers discover this book and decide if it's right for them.

Every review counts and makes a huge difference for independent authors like myself.

Thank you again for your support and for choosing to read this book. I hope you enjoyed Abby's story and the town of Sugar Creek and that you'll come back for another visit soon!

Also by Nova Walsh

The Sugar Creek Series

Death and Wedding Cake

Death and Peaches

Death and Fondue

Death and Blackberry Pie

Death and Divinity (Coming Fall 2024)

Christmas in Sugar Creek (Short Story Collection)

ABOUT NOVA WALSH

 Author Nova Walsh writes culinary cozy mysteries full of humor, shenanigans, and friendships that last a lifetime. She mixes in a healthy dose of amateur sleuthing, some slow-burn romance, and a pinch of comedy in every book she writes.

Nova is a former chef/caterer who still loves to cook but loves to write even more. She's an enthusiastic, if not totally successful gardener and loves puzzles, reading, and hanging out with friends.

Nova lives in central Texas with her husband, son, and two delightfully crazy pups. When she isn't writing, she's often cooking, gardening, hiking, or reading a good book with a pup by her side.

You can contact Nova at nova@novawalsh.com

Printed in Great Britain
by Amazon

47146306R00138